Have Mercy

Barbara Ann Whitman

Thanks for what
you do - and thanks
for reading!

Barbara Ann
Whitman

Visit our website at **www.StillwaterPress.com** for more information.

First Stillwater River Publications Edition

Library of Congress Control Number: 2017961788

ISBN-13: 978-1-946-30041-6

ISBN-10: 1-946-30041-1

1 2 3 4 5 6 7 8 9 10

Written by Barbara Ann Whitman

Design by Nathanael Vinbury
Published by Stillwater River Publications, Pawtucket, RI, USA.
The views and opinions expressed in this book are solely those of the author and do not necessarily reflect the views and opinions of the publisher.

Dedication

In memory of my mother, who always told me "You can do anything, if you put your mind to it."

Acknowledgements

I am eternally grateful for the patient support and encouragement of many. Thanks to the Fiction Writers group at Harmony Library, especially Pat Kenny. I am also indebted to Pamela Herman and Wes Maloney for consulting with me and sharing their expertise on some important details. Most of all, I am awed every day by the courageous resolve of foster children and the tender devotion of those who open their homes—and their hearts—to care for them.

Chapter 1 *Sisters*

Mercy's earliest memory was watching her mother fall from the second-story window of their apartment building, landing on the ground with a thud. Mercy, who was five years old at the time, had awakened to muffled shouting in the hallway outside the small bedroom she shared with her three-year-old sister. Soon, the yelling grew louder and was accompanied by banging that shook the walls. She recognized her mother's voice, but she sounded different somehow, in a way that scared Mercy. She was just about to start crying when her sister began to stir. Mercy swallowed her own fear because she did not want to frighten Lily. Together, the girls huddled by their bedroom window and looked out at the night as Mercy tried to distract the toddler. It was summer and the window was open, leaving only a screen between the two girls and the dark night. That's when they saw their mother appear, seemingly out of nowhere, and watched as she plummeted to the ground below, screaming all the way.

The rest of the night was a noisy blur, with policemen, fire trucks, and an ambulance. Mercy did not witness the rest of the unfolding drama. Her teenaged babysitter came into the bedroom and coaxed the girls away from the window. Downstairs, in the kitchen, the sitter made them cocoa while a nice police officer tried to talk to Mercy. He explained that the rescue squad was taking Mommy to the hospital, where doctors would make sure she wasn't hurt. Another policeman was talking to the babysitter, who was now shaking and had started to cry. This scared Mercy, too, because she had never seen her sitter be anything but calm and nice. Soon, the babysitter's mother arrived, rushing into the kitchen and hugging her daughter tight. Lily was running around in her footed pajamas and oblivious to the chaos. Some of the other policemen were playing with her and laughing. In that moment, Mercy felt very, very alone...

A telephone was ringing and Mercy started, jarring herself back to the present. She grabbed the phone, answering on the second ring, still breathless as she returned from the past. She never was much for talking on the telephone, even as a teen, so taking a job in customer service had been a questionable decision. But, at the age of eighteen, Mercy was required to find a job if she wanted to maintain her status in what she called "the program." Her social worker, who was usually a bitch, had actually taken Mercy to several job interviews one afternoon, stopping for lunch at a McDonald's. Most of the places they went were horrid and Mercy could never even imagine herself working at jobs like that. But this place was clean and did not involve dealing with other people, except on the telephone, so it was less intimidating. Mercy wasn't very tall and her slight build made her appear even younger than she was, a disadvantage when making a first impression. Her light brown hair was shoulder length and she usually wore it down, and tucked it behind her ears when she was nervous or uncomfortable, like that day. The social worker had really talked her up to the manager, which Mercy believed was the only reason she got the job in the first place. It had been surreal, listening to her social worker say all those nice things about her, using her professional voice—the one she only used in court before this. Her brown eyes opened wide and Mercy had to remind herself to close her mouth and stop gaping as the social worker used words like "responsible" and "motivated." Mercy felt like she was watching a movie for a few minutes there, instead of living in her own life.

The woman on the other end of the phone call had a question that needed to be transferred to another department, so Mercy hung up and sighed, trying to push away the anxiety she was feeling. It had been building ever since her last counseling appointment, when her therapist brought up the possibility of Mercy requesting her records from the Department of Child Services. Now that she was of legal age, Mercy was eligible to review what was known as her "history" in the social work field. It was something that she had never really thought about. Of course, there were huge gaps in her life time for which she had little or no memory. Like when she was at a sleepover one time... Mercy closed her eyes and remembered...

The girls were spread across the living room floor in their sleeping bags. Everybody was sharing their best Christmas morning stories. Most of the girls had vivid memories of how they discovered there was no Santa Claus. Kelly had snooped in her parents' closet and discovered all of her gifts and then feigned surprise on Christmas morning. Jackie's older brother had told her there was no Santa, for which he was severely admonished by their mother. Despite her denials and assurances, Jackie knew her brother had been right. When it was Mercy's turn to tell all, she had pretended to be asleep.

She couldn't tell them that she never believed in Santa because her presents came from a social worker, who brought them in big green trash bags in the trunk of her compact car. There was always a tag affixed to the tied end of each bag, bearing her name or Lily's. After the social worker was gone, Mercy's mother and her current boyfriend would get drunk and open all the presents. Some of them got broken and others were sold to neighbors so her mother could buy more vodka. One time, her mother traded a doll house that Mercy wanted so badly. She got food stamps for it. When Mercy cried, her mother asked her, "What would you rather do, play with a stupid little house or have food to eat?"

Nowadays, holidays were spent at the program, where Mercy lived with five other girls who were in similar situations. The house was pretty nice and some of the staff members were cool, especially the weekend team. Whenever a holiday approached, they were extra nice. Mercy figured they felt sorry for the girls because they had no family to return to for a big meal, no fancy clothes and no presents from Santa. Last year, on Thanksgiving, some of the staff cooked a turkey. Mercy thought it was sort of funny to see them pretending to be excited, when she knew they were not really happy at all, spending the day away from their own families. Welcome to my world, she thought, where pretending to be happy and normal was a full-time gig.

The rest of the workday was uneventful and Mercy grabbed her slightly tattered jacket, slipping out as quickly as possible at the stroke of 5:00PM. The cold, fresh air felt good on the short walk to the bus stop, where she waited for her ride home. She found her hat in a pocket and pulled it down over her hair to keep her ears warm. Tonight was movie night at the program and she hoped they had picked out something halfway decent. Staff was always so picky, denying any requests for movies that were in any way controversial or that might strike a chord with any of the residents. Given the variety of family issues represented, including arrests, drugs, and mental problems, this didn't leave much to be deemed "appropriate" by staff. Mercy sometimes daydreamed about the day when she might have her own place and be able to watch whatever movie she wanted without somebody flipping out. Like the time staff let them watch The Diary of Anne Frank. Mercy thought it was going to be boring and too much like a history lesson, but it turned out to be pretty good. But later that night, another resident had flashbacks and started cutting herself, so staff had to dial 911. They didn't realize that the girl had been locked in a closet at a young age while her parents got high. She had been forgotten until the next day, when the social worker came and took her away.

That's the problem with always having somebody else make your decisions for you, Mercy thought. They don't always think things through any better than you might do yourself. But, Mercy's social worker said that she was going to be making more of her own decisions, now that she was eighteen. To Mercy, it felt like she had always been a puppet, with someone else controlling the strings: first—her mother and her teachers, then—her social workers and judges and, now staff members at the program.

She entered the house through the backdoor and smelled dinner cooking–something Italian, Mercy guessed. The girls took turns planning and preparing meals. Last week, she and her roommate had put together Taco Night, which was a big hit with everyone, including staff. They had found an old Mexican straw hat in the basement and decorated it for a centerpiece. Making dinner was kind of fun, but Mercy couldn't imagine doing it every day. It took a lot of time and effort just to manage the weekly dinner assignment. But, she was hungry every day. Maybe living in the program wasn't all that bad, after all.

Chapter 2 Opening the Door to the Past

Mercy sat up in bed, shaking off the dream that woke her. The house was quiet and it took her a moment to remember that today was Saturday. But where were the other girls, including her roommate? The bed beside Mercy was empty and the program was eerily silent. She grabbed her robe and crept down the stairs. At the kitchen table, she found her favorite staff person, Kate, doing paperwork. Mercy suddenly remembered that today was the Job Fair, held twice a year in the local high school gym. Because she already had a steady job, she had been excused!

"Good morning," said Kate cheerily, glancing up from her papers. "I was beginning to worry that I'd have to wake you for your appointment!" Mercy tried to smile, but was thinking, *Appointment? What appointment?* Then, it came to her! Her weekly counseling had been rescheduled last Tuesday and was at eleven o'clock today! The butterflies returned to Mercy's stomach, since this was the session when she would begin to learn her "history." Kate did not seem to notice Mercy's internal confusion, so Mercy fixed herself some cereal and sat down. This was one time when she would be happy for the distraction of the other residents, but Mercy was stuck with only her own thoughts and Kate, who was preoccupied.

Last week, Mercy's social worker had visited her at the program. She said that Mercy's child protection records had been copied for her. All she had to do was sign the release request. "How do you feel about that?" the social worker had asked. Usually, Mercy hated those cliché sort of questions. But she saw an opportunity to put off the task of reading the details of her family's past, which was not going to be pretty. However, she did not want to completely give up on learning her history, either.

In response to the social worker, Mercy shrugged her shoulders and said, "I don't know. Whatever. It's cool, I guess." The social worker must have figured out that Mercy was not too keen on the idea because she didn't push the issue right away. They talked about some other, more current things, like work, before returning to the subject of the case record. "I know this is going to be hard," the social worker said, "and sometimes it might be sad or upsetting. But there must be things that have happened to you that you don't understand, because you were so young at the time. I think you are ready and I think you can handle this now, or I wouldn't be talking to you about it." Mercy did not know what to say—she was still not used to her social worker talking to her like a grown-up. She tried to remember what her therapist and she had decided to do when this sort of situation arose. Mercy knew she should name her feelings. "I guess I'm scared," she managed to mumble. To her relief, the social worker smiled and said, "Of course you are."

In the end, it was decided that Mercy would learn about her past gradually, with help from the social worker and from her therapist. She had signed the release request, as well as an updated release to allow the social worker to share information with the therapist. And now, today, was the day it would all begin!

Mercy did not even realize that she had finished her cereal and was staring at an empty bowl. Kate was talking to her and gather-ing up her paperwork from the kitchen table. "I'm going into the basement to check some supplies," Kate said. "Meet me back here at ten-thirty, okay?" Mercy agreed and headed upstairs to shower.

Once they were in the car and on their way to Mercy's appointment, Kate turned and said, "You're awfully quiet today—everything alright?" She had actually been thinking about her sister, but Mercy did not share those details with anybody. Instead, she replied, "Just tired, I guess," hoping that would be enough to allow her to return to her daydream. She had not seen or heard from Lily in about six months. Even the social worker did not know where

Lily was, since she had run away from her latest foster home. Lily had run away before, but this was the longest she had ever been missing. Mercy knew that her past was also her sister's. She wished Lily was here or, at least, somewhere safe. Maybe that would make learning their history a little easier.

Mercy took a deep breath and turned the door knob. The counseling agency's offices were quieter than usual because it was Saturday. There was no secretary and only two other people waiting for their names to be called. One by one, their therapists appeared, quietly escorting them back to their individual office spaces. Mercy liked her counselor well enough, but that had not always been the case. She had been sent to many different places over the years. Many of the therapists were nice, while a couple were downright creepy, but Mercy mostly thought it was a waste of time and only went because it was required by her social workers. Then, she met Leslie, her current counselor. Mercy was almost seventeen at the time and had just moved to the Independent Living program. Leslie seemed to know what to say in a way that did not make Mercy angry, like before. And she was honest. Leslie didn't twist information so the social workers had an "investigation." Best of all, Leslie had not moved, gone on maternity leave, or left the agency for another job. So they had been meeting every week for more than a year now.

Leslie settled into her usual chair and Mercy did the same, as was their routine. After the customary small talk, Leslie got down to business. "So, I talked with your social worker this week," she began. Mercy liked that Leslie always told her when she had talked with social services. "I know that you signed a release for your case record. I think that was very courageous and I am wondering how we can use our time here to help you with that process." Mercy was nervous—and a little angry that Leslie knew more about her past than she knew herself. "Did you read my records?" she accused. Leslie replied that she had not seen any case notes, but had received a call from the social worker, asking her to address the issue of the family history with Mercy. That was as far as things had gone. Mercy relaxed a little. "I don't know how to start," she told Leslie.... "I want to know what the records say, but then again—I don't." Leslie suggested that they begin with their own connection and the issues that brought Mercy to her office in the first place. Mercy would no doubt have more questions now than she did back then—questions that might be answered with information from the case record. This seemed easy to Mercy and a lot less frightening, so she agreed.

Opening her own folder where she jotted down notes during their sessions together, Leslie took out a sheet of paper called a genogram, which was a diagram, like a family tree. She had drawn it during their very first appointment, which was called an Intake. Since Mercy had provided the information herself, it was a little sparse at first. Leslie had added to it a few times, whenever Mercy had more information about a family member. There were periods of time when Mercy did not see her mother, for instance. Then, her mother would resurface, having completed a detox program and graduated with a new boyfriend in tow. Sometimes, her mother married the new beau, and Leslie would update the genogram to reflect this change.

But, what struck Mercy now was not her mother's name on the paper, with the various lines and arrows around it. It was her father who caught her attention. In contrast, his name was written in a square, with no additions or corrections. Little was known about him when Mercy started counseling here and that had remained unchanged. Her memory of him was dim, if she really recalled him at all. According to what her mother had told her, Mercy's father was gone by the time she could walk. Still, she had a vague image of him that might have been from an old photograph. Or, perhaps she was confusing him with her memory of Lily's father, who hadn't stayed around much longer. For the first time since she could remember, the knot that usually formed in Mercy's stomach when she thought about these things loosened. What she felt, instead, was new and perhaps even a little foreign. Her anxiety about her family history was replaced with the beginning of something like excitement. Maybe she was finally going to find out exactly who she really was.

Chapter 3 *This Changes Everything*

The rest of the counseling session went well and they talked about the transitions that Mercy was facing when she began therapy with Leslie. At that time, the court had terminated her mother's parental rights permanently and Mercy was free to enter a program designed to teach her how to live on her own. "My mother couldn't even be bothered to come to court," Mercy had told Leslie at the time. And, although she had sounded angry, her eyes filled up with tears. As the months passed, Leslie had helped Mercy find some peace with her mother's shortcomings. But she still longed for her and daydreamed about her return. She had learned to mostly look forward and set goals for herself. At the close of today's session, Leslie had suggested that Mercy think about some new goals, now that she was legally an adult and able to make decisions about her future. One of those objectives, Mercy knew, would be to find any family members who might be out there, including her mother, father, and her runaway sister, Lily.

When she returned to the program, the house was noisy with excitement as the other girls were getting home from the job fair. Lunch was underway in the kitchen and everyone was talking at once. Mercy went through the motions and tried hard to focus. What she really wanted to do was escape to her room and think about the possibilities that lay ahead of her. That's just what she did, as soon as the dishes were cleared. Luckily, her roommate was leaving on an overnight visit to her family, so Mercy soon had the room to herself. She sat back on her bed, against her pillows, and folded her legs up beneath her. "Where do I start?" Mercy muttered aloud, biting her lower lip in concentration. She wished it wasn't Saturday, because then she could call her social worker and ask about her sister and maybe about her mother's last known address.

Mercy knew the court published an ad in the newspaper everyday for three weeks before her last court hearing. It was in the hopes that her mother and father would see it and know about the hearing. If they did not show up, then the court could make a ruling without them. The judge had temporarily taken away their parental rights years earlier, but the social worker said they were being overly cautious so that the judge's ruling would be final this time. Her father never responded to the court and Mercy always told herself that he had just not seen the newspaper. She had no idea what her mother's excuse was.

She decided to call her social worker anyway and leave a message. This felt strange because Mercy usually waited for the social worker to call and track her down when a meeting was needed or some question had to be answered. Mercy left the number at the program and asked that the call be returned Monday, after she got home from work.

That night, Mercy thought about finding her father as she lay in bed awaiting sleep. Since she had no concrete memory of him, she had to make up his looks and his personality. She imagined that he might be handsome and married and living in a neat little house. Would his wife be happy to meet Mercy? *Would she even know about me?* she thought, feeling mild panic! For the first time, Mercy wished the weekend was over so she could get some answers to the questions that were mounting in her mind. Mercy closed her eyes and tried to remember the last time she saw her father...

She was five years old and was living in a foster home after the first time she had been taken from her mother. A social worker came for her and drove Mercy to the Child Services office, where she sat in a little room with some beat-up toys. The social worker sat in the doorway, in a hard chair, drinking coffee and writing notes. Mercy's father sat on a leather couch, covered in graffiti, and stared at his hands. He had awkwardly hugged Mercy when he arrived and he smelled of cigarettes. When the hour-long visit was over, Mercy continued to play on the floor while the social worker walked her father out. Even though the door was closed, Mercy heard raised voices and her father seemed to be shouting at the social worker. Mercy never saw her father again.

The following morning, Sunday, Mercy was lying in bed, being lazy, when there was a soft knock at her door. "Mercy are you awake?" It was Kate, back on duty for the weekend day shift. Before she could reply, the door opened a bit and Kate stuck her head inside. "There are two social workers from Child Services here to see you," Kate said. Mercy was confused and did not respond. She grabbed her sweats and hastily got dressed while Kate went downstairs to wait with the social workers.

Mercy could hear murmurs of conversation as she came down the stairs. Rounding the corner into the living room, she found two unfamiliar social workers, a male and a female, talking with Kate, whose face looked serious. She introduced Mercy to the pair, who were weekend hotline workers who said they knew Mercy's usual social worker. "We are here because we have news about your sister," began the young woman kindly. She explained that they had responded to a call during the night, from the hospital in town. "Lily is going to be okay," she said. But she had been living on the streets and using cocaine. "Lily is going to need to get some help." Mercy exhaled loudly she had not even realized that she was holding her breath.

Mercy plopped down on the couch beside the woman. "Can I see her?" she asked. The social workers exchanged a glance. "There is something else you need to know first," said the young woman. "Your sister was pregnant and the baby was born last night, eight weeks prematurely." Mercy felt like all of the air had been sucked out of the room. There was a roaring in her ears as she struggled to process this information. *Lily couldn't have a baby*, Mercy thought *Lily was only a child herself!*

But the reality was that Lily was turning sixteen at the end of the month. And now, Lily had a baby! Things had changed drastically since the last time Mercy saw her little sister.

Chapter 4 *Running from Reality*

The hospital lights were so bright that Mercy squinted as she walked toward the elevators, her social worker at her side. On the ride over from the program, Mercy had tried to learn more about her sister's baby, but had trouble forming questions. "Where will Lily live, now that she has a baby?" she asked. Mercy was surprised to find out that the baby was already in the custody of the state, because of Lily's running away and using drugs. The baby, a boy, weighed only three pounds. The social worker warned Mercy that the baby would look very small and probably have some tubes attached. "You won't be able to hold him just yet," the social worker said. Mercy imagined looking at the babies through a big window, like she had seen in countless television shows.

But nothing had prepared Mercy for the sight of such a helpless little creature, barely recognizable as a human being. There were eye patches covering the baby's eyes and skinny tubes going into his tiny nose. Wires were attached to his bony little chest. Monitors clicked a steady rhythm beside the clear bubble-like container where he slept. Mercy was stunned and couldn't move or even talk. Her social worker gave her a moment to take it all in and then suggested that Mercy sit down while she went to find the baby's nurse.

There was a wooden rocker beside the baby, where Mercy sat, looking around for the first time. It was a big room, with several other babies in the same sort of contraption, each with machines that ticked and whooshed. Most of the other babies had people around them, presumably parents, who cooed and fussed over them. Some of them were in open cribs and could be held or at least touched. They had stuffed animals perched nearby, or pictures drawn by older siblings. You could instantly determine each baby's gender by the displays of blue or pink around their space. Mercy turned her attention back to her sister's baby and was struck by the bleak contrast of his sterile, white surroundings. She was startled by a strange noise until she realized that it was her own voice. Mercy had started to sob.

In a split second, she was engulfed by nurses, her social worker, and some of the other parents, all of whom soothed Mercy with kind words. "It's okay, dear—take a deep breath," said a nurse who handed Mercy a small paper cup filled with water. Mercy restrained her crying and took a sip. The social worker put her hand on Mercy's shoulder and said, "Take a deep breath and come with me." She led Mercy from the room, taking her to a quiet waiting area, away from the babies. They sat on a couch while Mercy pulled herself together, becoming increasingly more embarrassed by her unforeseen meltdown. "I'm so sorry," the social worker said. "I should have realized how hard that would be and I should not have left you alone." The baby's nurse joined them and asked Mercy if she had any questions. Mercy did not trust her own voice and, besides, she had no idea what to ask, even though she wanted to know everything. Sensing her desperation, Mercy's social worker came to the rescue by asking, "How is the baby doing?"

The nurse assured Mercy that the baby was going to live, "even though all those tubes and wires look scary." She explained, "He is too small to breathe on his own, so a machine is helping him." Mercy learned that the three wires on the baby's chest and belly were monitoring his heart rate and a probe on his tiny foot was checking his oxygen level, all of which were consistent—a good sign. And he was getting food through a feeding tube that went into his nose. The clear plastic box, Mercy learned, was called an isolette, which controlled the air temperature. "Babies grow fastest if they are kept warm," the nurse explained. "When he is able to maintain his own body temperature, he will be moved to an open crib."

13

Mercy was comforted by the matter-of-fact way the nurse talked about these things. Finally, she found her voice. "Why are his eyes covered?" she asked. The nurse explained that premature babies sometimes have something called jaundice. It's because their bodies have trouble filtering some things from their bloodstream. It's treated by placing the baby under a special light and their eyes are covered as a precaution. "His eyes are going to be just fine," she said. The nurse encouraged Mercy to use the portals in the isolette to touch the baby, when she was comfortable doing so. "Your presence helps the baby grow and get strong," said the nurse, kindly. "Even while he is inside his special bed, you can still touch him and talk to him."

Mercy realized that the nurse always referred to him as "the baby" and asked, "What's his name?" The nurse replied, "The mother has not given him a name yet. In fact, we have not seen the mother since the baby arrived on our unit." For a moment, Mercy was confused. Then, she became worried for her sister. She had temporarily forgotten all about Lily, while being overwhelmed by the existence of the baby! The nurse excused herself to return to her duties and Mercy turned to her social worker with an inquisitive look. "Lily was here at the hospital overnight," the social worker began. "We can go upstairs and check .... But, the way I understand it, Lily tried to check herself out, against medical advice. She managed to sneak out of the hospital before security could stop her."

Lily was gone. Again. For the second time in as many days, Mercy felt the floor beneath her feet crumble away. Even though she was seated, Mercy grabbed the arm of the couch for support, as if she were falling. Then, she felt all of her senses shutting down, one by one, starting with her ability to feel anything at all. She went completely numb and did not even try to reply when the social worker kept asking, "Are you okay?" Mercy was aware that the social worker was talking to her, but she could not understand anything she was saying. It was like she was speaking to Mercy through a long tunnel. The next thing she knew, Mercy was up and walking down the corridor. And then she was moving faster, running toward the exit, rushing away from the social worker, the hospital, the baby, the nurse. All of it.

Mercy ran through the parking lot and down the street, no longer able to hear the shouting voices behind her. The only sound she heard was the thudding of her own heart and her sneakers slapping the sidewalk. By the time she slowed her pace to a walk, Mercy was not sure where she was. This was an unfamiliar part of town. And the daylight was fading. But she didn't care. It felt good to be away from everything. "Who needs it?" she asked herself. "Who needs the hospital, the baby, the social workers, the program and all Lily's crap?" Suddenly, her feelings were coming back and Mercy was filled with rage. She wanted to throw things or break something. She picked up two rocks and hurled them, as hard as she could, against a parked car. A voice in a nearby yard yelled, "Hey!" and Mercy was running again. She turned a corner and saw a public park ahead, making out the shapes of some swings and a basketball court in the near darkness. Entering through the broken metal gate, Mercy headed toward the swings and plopped down on the hard seat, gripping the cold chains for support against the night.

Chapter 5 *You Have the Right to Remain Silent*

"That's her. She's the one I saw throwing rocks at my car!" Mercy heard the gruff words in a dream as she shivered in the cold. She slowly opened her eyes and tried to make sense of the scene unfolding around her. *Why am I lying on the hard ground?* she wondered, squinting against the flashing red and blue lights that cut through the dark. A police officer led the angry man away, the one who was shouting at Mercy. Another officer held out his hand and Mercy took it as he lifted her to her feet. "Let's see some ID, young lady," he said, shining a flashlight up and down the length of Mercy's body, taking in her dirty jeans and unkempt hair. For a split second, Mercy reached for her pocketbook. Then the memory of the last few hours came flooding back. "I... I don't have it," she stammered. "I must have left it at the hospital." The police officer raised his eyebrows. "Escape from the hospital, did we? Turn around and put both hands behind your back. We're going to take a ride downtown where we can sort this all out." Before she knew what was happening, Mercy was in handcuffs and seated in the backseat of a police cruiser. The only sounds she could hear were muffled voices and a crackling police radio. The vinyl seat was cold and stiff. A familiar, empty feeling filled her. Mercy felt very, very alone.

At the police station, the officer led Mercy by the elbow into an interview room. Once she was seated in a hard chair, the handcuffs were removed. "Do you want something to drink?" the officer asked. His tone was still serious and all business, but Mercy detected a kindness in his blue eyes that wasn't there earlier. All her life, Mercy had heard terrible things about the police. Her mother always called them "pigs" and shouted nasty threats at them when she was being arrested. Mercy was afraid. The officer left her alone, promising he'd be right back. Mercy had to think fast. She knew she was in trouble, but she was too upset to think clearly enough to form a plan. The officer returned, placing a Styrofoam cup in front of her. "My name is Patrolman Mike Barnes. Why don't you start by telling me yours." The simple act of human gentleness caused Mercy to burst into tears, barely able to respond. She managed to get her name out before she began to shiver again. Barnes rubbed his hand over his face and exhaled. "How old are you, Mercy?"

"Eighteen."

"Where do you live?"

"At the shelter program on South Main Street."

"Why don't you tell me how you ended up in the park tonight," Barnes said tenderly.

Mercy told him the story, starting with the early morning visit at the program from the social workers who told her about Lily having a baby, to her visit to the hospital earlier in the evening. "I don't know what happened," she explained," But I just had to get out of there fast." She recounted her running away from the hospital. "It was like I was running blind, trying to forget everything I had just seen—Lily's poor baby, all alone with all those tubes," Mercy said, hugging herself. "I ended up at the playground, in the dark." Mercy now remembered how she had grown weary while sitting on the swing. She had taken off her hoodie and bunched it up to form a pillow beneath her head as she curled up against some boulders at the edge of the small park. "I must have fallen asleep. The next thing I knew, you were standing over me," she said.

Barnes had remained silent while she talked, pausing only to take a few notes. He was in his early thirties, Mercy guessed, with short brown hair and a handsome face. "Mercy," he began. "We got a call from a man who lives near the park. He said someone had run through the neighborhood throwing rocks. There was some damage to his car."

"I didn't mean to. I was just so pissed off about everything!" Mercy started to cry again. This time, she couldn't stop. She rested her forehead on the table in front of her, still hugging herself tightly. She was so tired of the whole thing. "My life sucks."

There was a soft knock at the door and a female officer tiptoed into the room, handing Barnes a sheet of paper. She left immediately and Barnes looked at the paper. "Well, you've never been arrested before. That's a good thing." He smiled at Mercy. "And a social worker did call to report you as a runaway this evening." Mercy's heart skipped a beat. "Am I going to jail?" she asked, feeling panic rise in her throat.

Barnes looked at her for a moment before answering. "Mercy, the man whose car was damaged wants to press charges. That would mean a Destruction of Property charge. Because you are eighteen, the matter cannot be handled in juvenile court, as a simple Runaway warrant. A judge will have to decide what happens next."

Mercy's heart sank. "But I didn't mean to do anything wrong. I was just mixed up from seeing the baby and Lily... Oh my God!" Mercy's eyes opened wide and she sat up straight. Suddenly, she remembered that Lily was missing. "I have to get out of here," she shrieked, standing up and knocking over her chair. "I have to find my sister!"

"Whoa there," said Barnes, standing across the table from Mercy. "You can't go anywhere until we get Child Services down here *and* talk to a judge." The female officer appeared again, as if by magic. "CS has been notified and will be sending someone over," she told Barnes, disappearing once again. Mercy must have looked confused because Barnes pointed to a small camera in the corner, up near the ceiling. The pieces fell into place as Mercy realized that they were being watched by other police officers, who had obviously checked her criminal record and sent the messages in to Barnes.

She was so overwhelmed by her situation that she swayed, feeling like she might faint. She gripped the edge of the table as Barnes came around the room, moving quickly. He took Mercy by the arm and led her out of the room and down the hall. The police department was quiet and dark, with only a couple of other officers present, working at their desks. The female officer followed, as if by some unspoken cue, and they entered a small room. There were two comfortable chairs and Barnes indicated that Mercy should sit, so she did. "This is Officer LaBelle," he said, pointing toward the other officer. "She will sit with you for a while." Barnes left the room, closing the door behind him. Mercy curled her legs up beneath her and leaned her head back against the chair's cushioned back. After several minutes, she gave in to the exhaustion that had been building all night and closed her eyes.

Chapter 6 Choices

Mercy woke up not knowing where she was for the second time in twenty-four hours, trying to identify the hushed voices outside the small room where she slept in a chair. There was a blanket covering her that she did not remember being there before. The door opened slowly and Officer Barnes came in, handing Mercy another Styrofoam cup, this time containing hot tea. Close behind him was Mercy's social worker. "What time is it?" Mercy asked, still trying to orient herself to the place and her situation. "Five-thirty in the morning," said the social worker, which explained her annoyed expression. "I was worried sick about you and called the hotline every few hours, all night. When the police called in to report that you'd been found, they agreed to let me come out instead of the emergency team." Mercy didn't know how to respond. As if things weren't bad enough, now she had everybody angry with her. "Can I go home?" she asked. "I really need a shower." It was Barnes who replied. "Not yet, Mercy. There are a few things that need to be ironed out first and they are going to take some time." He looked at the social worker, who continued to explain. "Officer Barnes has offered to talk with the man whose car you damaged and to ask him to drop the charges." Mercy felt a flicker of hope for the first time in days. "But," said the social worker, "we will need your cooperation on a few things first."

Here it comes, thought Mercy, steeling herself against whatever new demands the social worker had cooked up. But it was Barnes who explained the "deal," as he called it.

The case still had to go before a judge, since the charges were filed when Mercy was brought to the station. Barnes thought the car owner might be agreeable to having the charge dismissed, if Mercy agreed to pay for the damages to be repaired. "The judge will also have to be convinced," Barnes said. "But you've never been in trouble before, which helps. He might suggest some community service."

Mercy felt the glimmer of hope fade as she tried to imagine paying for the car damages while missing time from work to do community service. But she knew she had little choice, unless she wanted a probation officer, court fees, and all the things that went along with it. Mercy had grown up watching her mother go back and forth to court. *A lot of good it did her*, she thought.

"What choice do I have?" Mercy asked, shrugging her shoulders.

"Well," Barnes said, rubbing his face with his hand, "you can go before the judge and plead to the crime of Destruction of Property and hope he's in a good mood." He looked at the social worker again. She seemed to pick up on the idea and explained to Mercy that she probably would not be allowed to continue to live at the program, since having a criminal record is not permitted by residents. "Since you are legally an adult, I cannot provide a foster home anymore and you'd risk becoming homeless."

"Like I said," Mercy replied, "What choice do I have?" But she tried to give a small smile, feeling oddly confident that the two adults before her might actually be on her side, despite the grim picture they had just painted for her. Mercy thought she saw both Barnes and the social worker visibly relax. "Now that that's settled," Barnes said, "Let me see if I can get you some breakfast."

Once they were alone, the social worker looked at her, shaking her head. "I don't know what you did right in a previous life, Mercy," she said, "But I have never seen a kid treated so royally after being arrested!" She swept her hand around the room and continued, "A big chair, a blanket, and breakfast?" Mercy was shocked by the observation, but started to realize that maybe the social worker was right. Her experience was not like the horror stories she had heard from others. Through the years, growing up in the system, Mercy remembered many tales from other foster kids who returned after run-ins with police. They all seemed to describe being mistreated and disrespected. "Just lucky, I guess..." And with that, Mercy plopped down on the big chair and realized that she was starving.

After gulping down two donuts and an iced coffee, Mercy was allowed to clean up a little. The social worker went to the program and brought back some clean clothes, a toothbrush, and her hairbrush. Then, Mercy was led to a holding cell to wait for court. The police station was much brighter and noisier than last night, but the area where the cells were was quiet, leaving her alone with her thoughts. Mercy closed her eyes and remembered...

She was in the third grade the first time she remembered visiting her mother in jail. It had been awhile since she had seen her and she was really excited. Mercy could barely concentrate in school that day, except for art class, when she had been allowed to draw a special picture to take to the visit. Mercy had chewed her lip in concentration, her pigtails shaking as she vigorously colored in the pretty flowers she had drawn.

When the social worker picked her up from school, Lily was already buckled into her booster seat for the visit. Mercy rode sitting up as straight as possible, trying not to wrinkle the picture that she had refused to fold in half, not wanting to ruin it. She managed to keep her sister from grabbing it.

The prison looked like a haunted castle and had a tall fence all the way around it. Mercy and Lily held hands tightly while the social worker talked to a man behind a window with bars. A loud buzzing noise made them jump as the door slid open. The door slammed shut behind them and they followed the social worker down a very long corridor. They entered a big room with lots of tables and chairs. There were a few families visiting, talking quietly, coloring, taking photographs. There were two men watching from different corners. They were wearing uniforms and Mercy looked to see if they had guns on the belts, like on television.

Finally, Mercy saw her mother being led into the room by a woman in a uniform. She probably had a gun, too. They were all quiet at first, like they forgot how to talk to each other. Her mother looked mad and her hair was not the same color as Mercy remembered. Lily started to cry. The social worker put her hand on Mercy's back and said it was okay to hug her mother. She didn't really hug back, but put her arms around Mercy awkwardly, crushing the picture she had drawn. Mercy placed it on the table and her mother hardly seemed to notice before she started to light a cigarette. One of uniformed men came rushing over and Mercy was afraid she was in trouble. He told her mother, "No smoking in the visiting room!" Her mother put the cigarette away and started talking sort of mean to the social worker, saying things about her lawyer. Lily looked scared and crawled up into the social worker's lap. Mercy had wished she was younger so she could do the same thing.

Chapter 7 *This Can't Be Happening*

The memory of visiting her mother in jail was depressing and Mercy's spirits sank, as she sat alone on the hard bench in the bleak cell. She felt dirty, despite the clean clothing her social worker had brought for her. She was still shivering, but Mercy couldn't tell if she was cold or scared. Ever since she could remember, Mercy had tried to do the right thing and to please whomever was watching. It had been easy to fly under the radar because Lily always stole the show with her antics: first by being cute and innocent, when she was a toddler. Later, Lily garnered the attention by running away and using drugs. Meanwhile, Mercy was the one who ate strange food served at new foster homes and went to bed without complaining. She did her homework and graduated from high school. She entered the residential program and found a job. She had never really been in trouble. How had things gone so bad, so fast? she thought.

Because now, it was Mercy who was in serious trouble, and the feeling was foreign to her. She didn't know how to act or what to say and now she had to face a judge! And, most of all, she hated herself for screwing up when Lily was missing and there was a baby who was all alone in the hospital. A lot of use I am, Mercy thought, stuck in jail. And, Mercy didn't know if she would still be welcome at the program or if she was homeless. And what about my job? she thought. There were no more tears because she simply did not have anything left. Mercy hung her head in defeat.

She didn't even raise her head when she heard footsteps approaching the cell. The officer opened the door, using one of the many keys hanging from his belt. "Time to go, missy," he said, holding up a pair of handcuffs. Mercy stood and headed toward the door, still looking at her feet. Her humiliation was complete when she was led through the busy police department, her hands bound behind her in the cuffs. Outside, a windowless van was waiting at the curb to take her to court.

When they arrived at the courthouse, Mercy was led into another holding cell, not unlike the one at the police station. But this time, she had lots of company. The handcuffs were removed inside the cell and Mercy found a seat in the corner, where she could survey her new surroundings. There were four other women, all of them older. Nobody spoke to her but they all stared, not caring that Mercy caught them looking. She felt naked and thought she might throw up. Eventually, two of the women returned to a private conversation, talking in hushed tones. A third woman slouched down onto the floor and seemed to fall asleep sitting up, her back against the grey, concrete wall. The fourth woman sat opposite Mercy and cried quietly to herself.

Finally, a female court officer came for Mercy, leading her into the brightly-lit courtroom. They stopped at a long table facing the bench, which was empty with no sign of a judge. At the table, a man in a suit looked up from the papers he was reading and offered his hand. "I'm your court-appointed lawyer," he said in a friendly voice, "Attorney Miller." He indicated that she should sit beside him and Mercy did. Looking around the courtroom, she saw that her social worker was at another table, speaking with a young man, also wearing a suit. She couldn't hear what they were saying, but Mercy got the feeling they were talking about her, from the way they both kept glancing in her direction. This made her feel angry, but the lawyer started talking before she could react. "I've met with your social worker and the probation officer," he began. He opened a folder and took out some papers, which he said was the police report.

Mercy felt dizzy. So much was happening so fast! The new fact that she had a probation officer sickened her and reminded Mercy of her mother. She tried hard to concentrate on what her lawyer was saying. "I think if we agree to pay restitution, in addition to community service, the judge will allow you to return to your program. You'll have to meet with probation on a regular basis and obey the terms curfew, counseling, work. We'll ask that the charges be continued without a finding for six months and then, if you comply, we can ask that the charges be dropped." Mercy opened her mouth and was trying to formulate a question. Just then, a door in the front of the room opened and a loud voice commanded, "All rise!" Everyone stood up quickly and watched the judge stride into the room, wearing a black robe and a stern expression.

Besides his robe, his hair was grey and his blue eyes looked out at Mercy as the probation officer the man sitting with her social worker informed the judge of the previous night's events. Mercy was horrified to hear her behavior described in open court. She wished she could crawl under the table when the probation officer referred to the police report. "She was found sleeping in the park after fleeing from her social worker and throwing rocks at a parked vehicle." Her heart sank when the probation officer reported that the damages to the vehicle were estimated at $800.

Next, Attorney Miller stood up and spoke to the judge. He asked that Mercy be treated fairly, since this was her first offense, precipitated by a series of difficult and emotional events. He told the judge, "My client has agreed to terms of probation in exchange for being allowed to return to the community."

What? Mercy thought. *I agreed to what?*

She felt like her head was going to spin off her shoulders. It felt like a dream, watching and listening to complete strangers discussing her life, while she had no opportunity to say a single word. After her attorney sat down, her social worker stood and handed a written report to the court officer, who handed it to the judge. There was an uncomfortable silence while the judge read the report. When he was finished, he looked directly at Mercy for a moment. Her lawyer nudged her and motioned that she should stand. Mercy prayed that her legs would hold her upright. "How long have you been at your current program?" the judge asked.

"About a year, Your Honor," Mercy answered, like she had seen on television.

"Do you have a job?"

"Yes," Mercy replied. "I am a customer service rep at the mall."

"Do you agree to continue both the program and the job, as well as to stay out of trouble?"

"Yes, Your Honor," Mercy said with a trembling voice.

"Well, then, here's what we're going to do. You're going to go home and keep working. The man who owns the vehicle you damaged has agreed to allow you to pay for damages. You can meet with probation when we're finished and iron out the details. But I want you back in here in three months with a full report. Your probation officer will set up a schedule for your payments. And I think some community service wouldn't hurt, either."

Before Mercy could respond, her attorney stood and thanked the judge, indicating she was both agreeable and grateful. The judge banged his gavel and, in a booming voice, said, "The case is continued without a finding for three months and the defendant is released to the custody of the social worker."

Chapter 8 Home

Outside, Mercy gulped the fresh air and welcomed the warmth of the sun on her arms and face. In her sweaty hand, she gripped several pages of paperwork from the probation officer, and her lawyer's business card. Her social worker carried a plastic bag containing Mercy's dirty clothing—the outfit she was wearing at the time of her arrest. There was also Mercy's pocketbook, which she had left on the bench inside the hospital when she fled. Getting it back was like getting a bit of herself back and Mercy felt, for the first time, like this nightmare might be ending.

"Are you okay?" the social worker asked, genuine concern showing on her face.

Mercy struggled to find her voice once more, swallowing tears that threatened to erupt into a sob.

"Am I going home?" she asked tentatively. The social worker nodded and smiled. "That's the first time I remember you calling the program home," she said, "But I guess you'll be glad to sleep in your own bed tonight."

An invisible weight was lifted from Mercy's shoulders and she sat back against the seat of the social worker's car. But the relief was short-lived when she realized the meaning of the documents she now held on her lap. Her life was not her own, at least not for the coming months. She unfolded the contract she'd signed, labeled "Terms of Probation."

The social worker glanced over. Returning her eyes to the road, she said, "At least the guy's insurance is paying for most of the damage. You were lucky to get away with only repaying his deductible."

"But where am I going to get $250?" Mercy asked desperately. "That's a week's pay!" Before the social worker could respond, Mercy went on. "And how can I even work, when I have to find a volunteer job to qualify as community service?"

"I know it seems like a lot," the social worker replied, "but you have three months to pay the money, which is about $20 a week. And your community service is only 70 hours, which is about six hours a week you can do that on a Saturday."

Mercy was quiet for the remainder of the ride to the program. Kate greeted her in the front hall with a quick hug. Then she took a long look at Mercy. "We need to have a re-entry meeting, after all that has happened," Kate said, "but I think we can wait until tomor-row." The social worker nodded in agreement and told Mercy she would be back first thing in the morning.

As Mercy was climbing the stairs to her room, Kate said, "One more—thing you no longer have a roommate. Her plans to live with her grandmother were finally approved, while you were gone." Mercy was glad. Not that she minded having a roommate. But she just wanted to be alone tonight, and privacy was usually at a premi-um at the program. Still, the stripped bed and empty bureau struck Mercy as another sad event in her miserable life. She dropped her things on the vacant bed and flopped, face first, onto her own.

When Mercy opened her eyes again, the room was aglow with soft light. She was disoriented and did not immediately know what time it was or what day, for that matter. She was still dressed, but her shoes had somehow been removed and a blanket thrown over her. She stumbled out of the room and headed downstairs. Her confusion continued when she found Kate in the kitchen, knowing her evening shift would have ended hours ago.

"Well, look who's up!" Kate said brightly. "And just in the nick of time because your social worker will be here any minute." Apparently, Mercy's bewilderment was obvious, because Kate continued. "Nobody could wake you for dinner, so we just let you sleep through. My replacement got here an hour ago, but I wanted to stay for your re-entry meeting....you looked pretty rough last night."

"Thanks," Mercy said, making herself a cup of tea. She was hoping that the tea and a quick shower would clear the rest of the cobwebs before her social worker arrived and the saga of the previous days continued.

But once in the shower, Mercy's mind began to operate. She realized, with a feeling of panic, that she had missed two days of work. Dressing quickly, she returned to the kitchen just as her social worker arrived. Kate led them to a small conference room and closed the door. Mercy took a deep breath as the social worker opened a folder and withdrew several pages. "I rewrote your Service Plan," she began, "to include the terms of your probation. Some of this was already in place, Mercy, so it's nothing you can't handle."

Mercy felt a bit of relief and reached for a copy of the new plan. She would meet with the probation officer every two weeks, and he would come to her at work, during her lunch break. Mercy's counseling appointments had become infrequent during the past month, but she would now be seeing Leslie weekly. "What about community service?" Mercy asked. "I wouldn't even know where to start."

"I have some ideas," the social worker said. "Actually, I made a couple of calls this morning. I left a message for the hospital social worker, asking if there might be a position available for a Saturday volunteer." The social worker's voice trailed off and a small smile worked at the corners of her mouth. It took Mercy a moment to connect the dots and then she exclaimed, "The baby! I would be able to visit Lily's baby!"

The social worker held up a hand, as a caution. "Don't get your hopes up just yet. I'm not sure how they are going to feel about you after the commotion you caused. But it's worth a try."

For the first time in days, Mercy smiled. Maybe this community service gig was not all bad. And seeing Leslie every week was okay, too, except for the time out of work. "Work!" Mercy blurted, remembering her earlier panic over missing two days.

"I called them the morning after you ran off," the social worker said, "and your supervisor was very nice about it. I called again once we knew you were alright and they are expecting you to return to work after this meeting."

Kate had been listening to the exchanges and it was finally her turn. "The program is glad to have you back, Mercy, even under the circumstances. You have never given us any worries before and I trust that you won't pull any more stunts. We are willing to support the rules set up by the court. But I cannot promise you things will go this smoothly in the future, if there is another incident like this one."

"I get it," Mercy replied emphatically. "I think I am going to be way too busy to get into any trouble, anyway. I just want the next three months to be over and done."

"You can start by getting to work," the social worker said. "I'll even give you a ride and save you bus fare."

"But can we stop for lunch? I am starving!" Mercy pleaded.

"Now you're pushing your luck," the social worker said, rolling her eyes. But her smile told Mercy things were getting back to normal.

Chapter 9 *There's a New Kid in Town*

The next couple of days went by uneventfully, for which Mercy was grateful. After all of the recent drama, it felt good to have her normal routine back. Work was even a little slow, giving her time to think about everything that had happened. Mercy had caught up on her sleep and even rearranged her room, putting an old comforter on the empty bed left behind by her roommate. She knew from experience that the bed would not remain empty for long, but, for now, she was enjoying the privacy.

When it was time for her long-overdue counseling appointment, Mercy was unusually apprehensive. Normally, she didn't mind the sessions—in fact, she had grown to almost enjoy her fifty minutes of Leslie's undivided attention. But today, Mercy resented having to revisit the events from the previous week. The dust had settled and she wanted to move forward and forget about it. Besides, she knew that she was going to have to hear about how she had missed two weekly appointments prior to all of that, a point her social worker had already made, *ad nauseam*.

"A lot has happened since we last met," Leslie said. "I called your social worker to ask about the missed appointments and she filled me in, briefly."

"Did she say anything about Lily?" Mercy asked anxiously. She had left two messages for her social worker, but the calls were unanswered.

"No," Leslie said slowly, "but it's not my place to collect information about your sister. My role is to assist and support you."

"Well, you can help me by finding out where Lily is," Mercy said, "because that's all I care about right now!" She stared hard at her therapist and folded her arms across her chest.

Leslie met the challenge unflinchingly. "I understand that you are very worried about your sister. But I'm not sure how we can use your time here to change Lily's circumstances."

"Well, it's all I can think about, so maybe this is just a waste of time." Mercy hated it when Leslie tried to change the direction of the conversation by being so calm and rational. She wasn't going to let her off that easily.

"Suppose Lily was found today," Leslie said. "Can you think of anything that you could be doing that would be helpful to her?"

"I could take care of her baby!" Mercy shut her mouth. Until she blurted it out, she had not planned to say it. She had not even thought it. But, Mercy felt the thought taking root somewhere deep inside of her and she knew it was more than a fleeting idea.

"Okay," said Leslie. "Let's talk about that. Tell me about the baby."

Mercy told her all about the baby, recalling everything she had learned from the nurse that night, before she ran from the hospital. In the process, she told Leslie most of the details of the events that followed. The therapist let her talk, nodding here and there and asking an occasional question. When she was finished, Mercy took a deep breath. "And now, I don't know what to do next."

Leslie suggested that Mercy speak with the hospital to see if she might visit the baby to learn more about his progress and his care. Mercy looked grim. "I'm not sure they'll want me back there, after what happened. But my social worker might get me to volunteer there, as my community service for court."

"Perhaps you can advocate for yourself instead of leaving it all up to her," Leslie said. "I'd be willing to write you a recommendation and I'd bet your boss would do the same. And maybe someone at the program."

"Maybe I can fill out an application," Mercy said, "so they can know more about me."

"Sounds like you are starting to make a plan," Leslie said. "Let me get my laptop and I'll write up that recommendation for you right now."

By the time Mercy left the counseling agency, it was getting dark outside. She hoped that she hadn't missed the bus. Now that she had a curfew, there wasn't much time to waste between work and the program. And, if she was going to be asking people to write her letters of recommendation, she couldn't very well be showing up late for things. But the bus screeched to a halt at the curb, right on time. Mercy found a seat and thought about whom she would ask for the letters. Kate was her first choice at the program, although she had been the staff member involved in the running-away fiasco and Mercy feared she might see her differently now. But Kate knew her the best, of all the employees at the program. Her next shift wasn't until the weekend. Meanwhile, Mercy decided, she would ask her manager at work. Hopefully, the two and a half days she had missed last week would not count against her.

She arrived back at the program with twenty minutes to spare. Mercy went looking for a staff member to check in, following the sound of voices from the kitchen. There, she found the staff supervisor as well as an unfamiliar face. "Oh, good, you're here," said the supervisor. "Mercy, I'd like you to meet your new roommate, Jess."

The two girls exchanged awkward greetings. Just then, the kitchen door burst open. A harried woman of about thirty with wild blond hair dropped a bag on the floor at Jess's feet. "Here's the rest of your stuff," she said, breathlessly. "I've got to run, late for my next appointment. Don't let me get any phone calls about you, now." The woman pointed at Jess before turning and running out the door just as quickly as she had come in.

"Who was that?" Mercy asked, suppressing a smile.

"That," Jess said, "was my social worker." The three young women burst out laughing, breaking the tension that had started long before Mercy arrived home.

Mercy had taken a step backward to avoid the contents of the new girl's bag that had spilled out when the social worker dropped it. Now, she started to bend down to help retrieve the items that scattered across the kitchen floor. But Jess barked at her. "It's okay! I've got it!" That's when Mercy caught a glimpse of something very shiny. As the strands of braided gold were swept into the bag, Mercy saw that there were little price tags affixed to them with pieces of string. There were also three small velvet boxes. She stood up quickly, pretending not to notice. Apparently, the supervisor did not see it. She had been too distracted by the social worker's abrupt exit.

"Why don't you show Jess your room?" the supervisor asked Mercy, "and I'll see who's in charge of dinner tonight."

Chapter 10 Community Service

After dinner, the girls returned to their room. Mercy expected Jess would unpack her belongings. Instead, they remained in the big plastic trash bag. Jess said she was too tired, but spent a lot of energy rooting around inside the bag each time she needed something, like her pajamas or her toothbrush. Mercy had hoped that the unpacking might reveal some logical explanation for what she had seen downstairs, but her new roommate's behavior only increased her suspicions. To make matters worse, Jess went to a lot of trouble hiding the bag in the back of the closet before the girls left the room for the evening, heading downstairs to watch a movie.

The next day, Mercy had a busier than usual shift at work. There were a lot of disgruntled customers calling all day long with odd questions. Mercy's boss had wondered aloud if there was a full moon. But he was happy to write the recommendation that Mercy asked for, and she picked it up before leaving for the day.

After work, she had gotten off the bus two stops early. Mercy went to the hospital and asked for an application for volunteer work. Luckily, she did not see anyone who might recognize her from the incident. She got out of there as quickly as possible and walked the rest of the way home.

She had not given much thought to her qualms about Jess until she returned to the program. Mercy saw that all of Jess's things had been unpacked and very neatly put away. She didn't have much—just some clothes, bathroom items, and some makeup. There was no sign of the questionable items. And no sign of Jess.

"Mercy! Phone call!" shouted one of the residents from the hallway. Mercy ran down the stairs and took the call in the office, as was the custom in the evenings, closing the door for privacy. It was her social worker. "I'm sorry not to have returned your calls before now," she said, "but I was waiting until I had sorted some things out and had something concrete to tell you." Mercy plopped down in the desk chair and waited.

"Do you remember that police officer .... Barnes?"

"I'd rather forget him, and that entire night," Mercy said, rolling her eyes to the empty room.

"Well, don't write him off so fast," the social worker said. "He called me about another case the other day and, before he hung up, he asked me about you. Apparently, you made quite an impression. He was wondering how things had gone in court and if you were still living at the program."

"Great," Mercy said. "Now I have a police stalker."

"While I had him on the phone, I picked his brain about community service for you. I mentioned that I had called the hospital about a position there. That's when he told me that he works a couple of nights a week in the ER, doing a security detail."

"What?"

"Mercy, he offered to supervise you while you do community service there, if the hospital would approve. So, I talked to the hospital administration. And they agreed!"

Mercy couldn't speak. It was a shock to receive good news and have things go so incredibly right, for a change. She took a deep breath and managed an "Oh... my God!" so her social worker would know she was still on the line.

"Barnes is filling out the paperwork for Probation, but that's no big deal, seeing that he is a police officer. You will also have to fill out an application and provide references. Can you manage that?"

Mercy put a hand to her forehead, as if to control the thoughts that were bouncing around inside. "I already have!" she practically shouted into the phone, her excitement building as the pieces fell into place. "I picked up the application today and I have two recommendations, so far."

"Wow!" said the social worker. "Then you can meet with the hospital staff and work out a schedule that overlaps with the police detail. And Mercy? Nice job."

"Thank you," Mercy managed, tearing up. She couldn't believe that she was going to be able to see Lily's baby. She bounced out of the office and ran into Kate, who was just arriving for her Friday night shift at the program.

"Hey! What's the hurry?" Kate asked. Mercy was beaming and she blurted it all out, happy to have found someone with whom she could share the news. She followed Kate back into the office, talking the whole way.

After congratulating Mercy, Kate said, "I hear you got a new roommate."

Mercy felt like she'd been punched, as her joy quickly turned to anxiety and her worries about Jess became front and foremost. "Yes," she said, trying to maintain her smile. "But I haven't seen her today. I think I'll go look for her. See you later!"

Mercy took the stairs two at a time and entered the room just as Jess shrugged off her jacket and fell onto the bed. "My social worker is the biggest piece of shit that ever lived!" Jess told Mercy. "I had to go to Juvenile Court today. And I was there *all* day because that lazy bitch forgot to show up. And now, I have to go back again tomorrow!"

"Oh... why were you in court?" Mercy asked. She was glad that Jess had her face buried in her pillow and could not read the dread on Mercy's face.

"I was supposed to have some shoplifting charges dismissed, so I can stay in this program. If she doesn't show tomorrow, I swear...."

Just then, there was a knock at their door and someone yelled, "Dinner!" Mercy had never been so happy to hear that word, even though she was sure she'd have no appetite.

Chapter 11 Compassion Will Only Get You So Far

Mercy was running down a steep hill, gaining speed, and unable to stop. She was swerving to avoid trees and rocks that suddenly appeared in her path. She could hear someone crying the soft sobs coming to her on the wind. Gradually, she struggled awake and realized she had been dreaming. But the crying continued. Mercy switched on the bedside lamp and looked over at her roommate. Jess was curled in the fetal position, holding a pillow over her face. "Are you okay?"

Jess reached for a tissue and blew her nose before answering. "Sorry. I woke up and didn't remember where I was. Then I started thinking about court tomorrow and how I miss my brothers and how much I hate starting over again at a new school...." Jess cried harder, burying her face back in her wet pillow.

Mercy gave her a few minutes to get it all out while she thought about what she should do. The feelings Jess was experiencing were nothing new to her, so she knew the deal: Jess would put on a brave face tomorrow and deal with the changes in her life. It was somehow easier in the light of day. But, at night, reality always looked more hopeless.

When the sobbing subsided, Mercy got Jess some water and clean tissues. "Where are your brothers now?" she asked.

"Nobody knows where Derek is. He turned eighteen three foster homes ago and took off. Bobby and I got to stay together at the next place—he's only twelve. But our foster father was a prick and hated me. After I got arrested, they threw me out, but kept Bobby. I went to a locked facility and by the time I got out, they had adopted Bobby. Yesterday, my piece-of-shit social worker told me that they won't let me see him and there's nothing she can do about it. As if she would, anyway."

Mercy wanted to know more about the arrest but didn't want to ask about it directly, fearing Jess would be suspicious that she knew about the things she had hidden somewhere in the very room they shared. Instead, she asked, "Do you think they might change their mind after your charges are dismissed?"

Jess shook her head. "It's not like it was all my fault. They wouldn't give me money for things, even though the state pays them and the money was really mine. I mean, I needed new boots, so I took the money from his wallet while he was sleeping. When they searched my room, *my* personal things, they found some other stuff that I couldn't explain. So they just called the police and didn't even care that Bobby was right there, crying while they took me away. That's the last time I ever saw him."

"What about your real parents?" Mercy asked tentatively.

Jess snorted. "My father's in jail for trying to kill my mother. That was the first time we got taken away. But definitely *not* the first time he tried to kill her. But she always lied about it and made us lie, too, so they couldn't really do anything. We lived with our mother again after that, but she kept letting her new boyfriend beat her up. Derek used to fight with him, too, and one time he went to school with a black eye. We weren't about to lie and protect that asshole...especially after he started hitting Bobby. But the social workers still blamed my mother and we were taken away again. The rest is history."

The girls talked until the sky started to brighten, then Mercy dozed off. When she awakened, Jess was gone. She had to hurry so she wouldn't miss the bus and be late for work. Mercy felt badly for Jess especially the part about her brothers. She worried about Lily every day and every night, too. But at least now she had the baby. Jess had no one.

That night, Mercy was tired because she got so little sleep the night before. Jess was in a foul mood, angry about whatever had happened in court. Mercy avoided her roommate as much as possible and went to bed early, falling into a deep sleep.

In the morning, Jess was still miserable and grumbling about her first day at the local high school. Mercy learned that the judge had refused to dismiss the shoplifting charges, jeopardizing Jess' continued placement at the program. She tried to eat breakfast, but Mercy had a knot in her stomach again, thinking about the open charges and the still mysterious items in Jess' possession, hidden somewhere in their room...... in *Mercy's* room!

All day, the situation nagged at her. She couldn't help but feel sorry for Jess. A lot of bad things had happened to her that were not her fault. Mercy chewed her lip until it bled, as she was reminded of how angry she used to be about her own crappy life. But she wasn't so angry any more—at least not most days. But, if she was right about Jess having stolen goods in their room, it might not end well. Could Mercy be blamed for knowing about it? Could she trust her roommate to own up to it, if the goods were discovered? It dawned on Mercy that what she was feeling was fear. Things were just starting to go her way and she was supposed to meet the hospital staff tomorrow, to work out her volunteer schedule. She couldn't let Jess screw that up for her. Mercy needed a plan.

Chapter 12 Secrets

When she got home from work, Mercy went straight to her room. Jess was not home, so she had the place to herself. She plopped down on her bed and looked around. This was the one place Mercy had finally been comfortable enough to call "home," where she felt safe. But that had changed, thanks to Jess. Mercy wanted to take matters into her own hands, but first, she needed to know exactly what she was dealing with. She took a deep breath to fortify herself and opened Jess's closet. There wasn't much to see—just a couple pairs of shoes on the floor and a few shirts on hangers. Standing on tiptoes, Mercy saw nothing on the top shelf except some dusty books. She reached up with her hand and swept the rear of the shelf, where she couldn't see. In the corner, her hand found plastic. It was the trash bag that held the sum of Jess' belongings on the day she arrived at the program. Remembering what she'd glimpsed that day, Mercy patted the bag and felt something inside, then pulled her hand back as if she'd burned it. She stood still and listened carefully. The program was quiet, only distant voices drifting up from the first floor, where dinner was being made. Mercy reached up again and pulled the bag down from the shelf.

Emptying the contents onto her bed, Mercy stifled a gasp. Her worst fears were confirmed as she gazed down at the goods: there were several gold necklaces, with little price tags affixed to each, the least expensive being more than a hundred dollars. There were also numerous velvet boxes that she was too afraid to open. She shook the bag again and out dropped three unopened DVDs. Exhaling a breath she hadn't realize she was holding, Mercy whispered, "Oh my God!" to the empty room. Then, she quickly stuffed the items back into the trash bag, barely touching them, as if they were toxic. She scrunched the bag into a ball and shoved it back into the corner of the closet shelf, as she had found it, and closed the door. She felt like throwing up.

Mercy sat on the bed again but the adrenaline pumping through her veins made it impossible to stay there. She paced the room and tried to think what do next. She looked at her phone, wanting to tell someone, but who would she call? She couldn't tell anyone who would act officially yet—she needed to think things through before starting something she wouldn't be able to control. Mercy thought of Leslie and remembered that she had a counseling appointment later in the week. But she honestly didn't think she'd last that long without having a heart attack or something. She called and left a message, asking the therapist to call back about an emergency appointment.

Mercy was distracted at dinner, but glad that she was not alone when Jess arrived home, in the middle of the meal. She was able to avoid her roommate without it being too obvious. And Jess had clean-up duty, allowing Mercy to slip away unnoticed as soon as she was finished eating.

Her cell phone was ringing when Mercy returned to her room, answering with a breathless, "Hello?"

"It's Leslie—is everything alright?"

Mercy relaxed. "I need to talk to you right away, like tomorrow. Please tell me you have an opening."

"Well…" Leslie hesitated. "I am pretty booked. But maybe we can meet at lunchtime, if it's important?"

"Yes!" Mercy said. " I am meeting with the hospital social worker in the morning, so I am not going into work until the afternoon. Can I come at noon?"

"That will work," Leslie said, "as long as you don't mind me eating my lunch while we talk."

"See you then, and thanks." Mercy hung up and sighed, feeling relieved to have taken a step toward dealing with the situation. She felt her heartbeat returning to normal for the first time all day. But, now that she knew for certain what was hiding in her room, things still felt a lot more urgent.

Jess was talkative again that night, as they went through their evening routines and got into bed. She didn't seem to realize that Mercy was distant. She complained about school and her social worker, while Mercy pretended to read a magazine, propped up on her pillow. She felt that she couldn't return her roommate's friendly chatter without sounding fake and giving away what felt, to Mercy, like her betrayal. Eventually, Jess drifted off to sleep and Mercy tried to do the same, turning off the bedside lamp.

Mercy closed her eyes and remembered..... the last time she had shared a room with Lily, in a foster home. Lily, at 13, had come home past curfew again. Their foster parents were worried and upset, but mostly they were angry. Lily had laughed and sneered as they tried to talk to her, threatening to call the social worker in the morning and terminate the placement. Mercy knew that meant the sisters would be separated. But she couldn't defend Lily's behavior, at least not while she was slurring her words and muttering "whatever" as their foster mother was in tears. That night, Mercy didn't sleep at all, worrying about what would happen next. After school the next day, she looked for Lily as usual, but she was nowhere to be found. Mercy rode the school bus home without her sister, wondering what she would tell their foster parents when she arrived alone. But when she walked in the door, she found their social worker in the kitchen, looking serious. Lily had left school without permission, and was missing. A search of her locker revealed some makeup that had been stolen from a store at the mall. The social worker was asking for permission to search the room the sisters shared and she eyed Mercy suspiciously, as if she expected her to object. The foster mother agreed to the search, adding that the social worker might as well take Lily's belongings while she was at it, because she would not be welcomed back. Mercy felt completely helpless.

The last thought Mercy had before falling asleep was that she would not simply stand by, while the world crumbled beneath her feet again. Not this time. Not ever.

Chapter 13 *Finding Direction*

Mercy fidgeted on the hard bench in the hospital corridor, where she waited for her appointment with social services. The noisy chaos somehow soothed her. The air of life and death struggles around her put Mercy's own worries in perspective. Lost in a day-dream, Mercy felt a shadow cast over her and looked up. Officer Mike Barnes was smiling down at her. "A penny for your thoughts," he said. Mercy brightened and returned his smile. "I'm here to arrange my volunteer schedule," she said.

"I know. I had a message asking me to drop off my schedule for the coming week, so they can match our time, since I'll be supervising you." He handed Mercy a sheet of paper. "I guess you can deliver it for me. But stop and see me before you leave. I'll be here until one o'clock and then I'll be heading to the police department for my regular job."

The meeting went well and Mercy arranged to volunteer two days a week one evening and Saturdays. She asked about Lily's baby and the news was good. He was not yet breathing completely on his own, but there were no drug withdrawal symptoms and he had gained several ounces. But he was still very small and being monitored. If Mercy's shifts went well, she would be allowed to visit the baby for a half-hour at the end, as long as Officer Barnes was available to be on the ward. There had been no sign of Lily, the social worker said, and human contact was a very big part of the baby's survival. Tears stung Mercy's eyes as she recalled the cold, bleak corner of the unit where the baby slept. The social worker agreed to accompany her upstairs for a brief visit, since she was on her way there for a meeting anyway. In the elevator, Mercy silently summonsed the courage to see the baby again without falling apart this time. She was relieved to see Barnes chatting with the nurses behind the desk. He gave her a wave and then caught up with them as they walked toward the baby's room. The social worker saw Barnes and said, "I'll go ahead and let the nurse know you're coming." Then she clicked her heels down the hall and disappeared, leaving them alone.

"She's all business," he told Mercy, watching the social worker disappear, "but you'll love the nurses on the floor. They're really great." He took Mercy's elbow and steered her into the baby's room. Barnes introduced her to the nurse in charge of Lily's baby.

Mercy had to scrub her hands and slip a hospital gown over her clothing before approaching the isolette. Her stomach was tied in knots again. But she relaxed when she saw him. The baby already looked bigger and seemed stronger, less fragile. Not only that, but the patches had been removed from his eyes. Despite the presence of wires attached to his torso, he was more easily recognizable as a member of the human species. The nurse showed her how to place her hands inside the two special holes provided that allowed Mercy to touch the infant.

"He may not react to your touch," the nurse told her, "but he knows you are here and it stimulates his instinct to thrive. It's very important that he have a chance to bond with another human being if he is going to continue to grow."

This all sounded pretty complicated to Mercy, who was too nervous to really understand what the nurse was saying. But she followed directions and slipped her hands into the isolette. It was warm inside and Mercy tentatively stroked the baby's tiny forearm. Then, she placed a finger into his tiny palm and the baby closed his fist around it. Everything else ceased to exist for a moment as she felt the first physical connection between herself and this peculiar little person who was her nephew. But instead of feeling overwhelmed, Mercy felt changed in some endless way that could not be measured. She knew it was right and she knew what she had to do.

Chapter 14 An Idea

Before she could formulate how she would tell him about the stolen jewelry, Barnes was called away when his name was paged on the hospital intercom, and he did not return. Mercy was disappointed to have missed the chance to unburden herself and worried that she might lose her nerve. But if she waited for him, she would miss her counseling appointment. Her resolve strengthened as she walked the three blocks to Leslie's office and thought about her time with the baby.

Leslie ate a sandwich from a brown bag while Mercy talked. Usually, the therapist remained neutral and murmured appropriately when Mercy rattled on. But today, Leslie's eyes grew bigger as Mercy described what she had discovered in her roommate's closet. "I feel sorry for Jess, really," Mercy said. "She doesn't have any family to visit her and her social worker is pretty clueless..."

"But...?" Leslie prompted.

"But I don't want to sit back and do nothing and then wish I had done something, when it might be too late," Mercy said. "And I want to do what's right for Jess. But it's my room, too, and those things are freaking me out. Can I get in trouble just for knowing about it?"

"I guess it's possible," Leslie said, between bites. "At the very least, it might take some sorting out to determine who is responsible. It complicates things now that you know about the stolen goods being in your room."

"Oh, God," Mercy groaned. "What am I going to do?"

Leslie suggested that Mercy go to the police station to seek out Barnes' opinion. But Mercy had to work and had already missed enough hours, with the court-ordered restitution payments still looming. By the time she finished, Barnes' shift would have ended too. There was no way Mercy was waiting until tomorrow. "I can't take another night in that room," she said.

"Let's hear what you would say to him, if Barnes was here right now," Leslie said.

Mercy chewed her lip for a few seconds and then blurted the whole business out. She began with Jess arriving at the program and spilling her bag on the kitchen floor, when Mercy caught a glimpse of the shiny gold chains. Her suspicion grew as she learned of her roommate's history, she said, and her court case. She finished with her discovery in Jess' closet the previous day. Leslie nodded approvingly of Mercy's ability to recount the steps that led her to this point. Then she said, "I have an idea."

Leslie wanted Mercy to write down everything she had just told her and then sign her name with today's date. "Then I'll sign it too," she said, "as a witness." Mercy started to object, but Leslie held up her hand. "Let me finish. I will seal the letter in an envelope and keep it for as long as you want or destroy it if you tell me. Or deliver it to the police department or the program staff if that's what we decide together."

"But why can't you just tell them if something happens or show them your notes or something?" Mercy asked.

"Because it becomes very complicated when a therapist has to divulge information like this, Mercy, and session notes are not always admissible as evidence. My motivation and reputation, and yours, would be called into question. We'd have to answer a lot of questions and your message might get lost in the translation. But a written document would be your insurance policy while you decide your next step."

So, Mercy wrote it all down, carefully rechecking her words and including all the facts. Leslie left her alone with the task while she made some phone calls, returning as Mercy finished writing.

They both signed and dated it and then placed in an envelope, securing the seal. Leslie placed it inside her binder, with her notes from today.

Mercy had to hurry to get to work by one o'clock, as she had promised. She sat on the city bus, her head against the cold window, watching the blur of passing cars. Mercy hoped she was doing the right thing. She was filled with excitement from being with Lily's baby. She was scared about the note in Leslie's office. She was sad about betraying her roommate. But one thing was certain: nobody could accuse her of standing by while life happened around her. Mercy bounded off the bus with a spring in her step and a small, tight smile on her lips.

Chapter 15 Visiting Hours

The rest of the afternoon was uneventful and Mercy was grateful. She'd had enough drama for one day and was so exhausted that she fell asleep after dinner. She awoke before the alarm the next morning and headed to work early. She figured it wouldn't hurt to make up some of the time she had lost the day before, when she'd been at the hospital and seeing her therapist. It also didn't hurt that she would avoid seeing Jess again. Mercy felt like she was keeping a big secret—and, in a way, she was. But the real secret belonged to her roommate and Mercy wondered how Jess could be so calm, knowing what she was hiding. She guessed that Jess had had a lot of practice at being deceitful, which worried Mercy even more.

When five o'clock rolled around, she headed to the hospital for her first volunteer shift of community service. Officer Barnes was doing an evening security shift in the Emergency Room, so that's where Mercy was assigned. She even got an official-looking name tag that identified her as a volunteer. At first, the staff seemed perplexed about finding something for her to do. But it was eventually decided that she would shadow the triage assistant, helping patients and their family members get settled after they had checked in and provided insurance information. Mercy gave them plastic bags for the patient's belongings and showed whoever accompanied them where the waiting lounge was, in case they needed a restroom or a vending machine. It was slow in the beginning, but things picked up and Mercy found the time flew by quickly. She barely had time to grab a burger from the cafeteria during her short break.

When her shift ended, Mercy found her way to the newborn intensive care unit. Barnes agreed to meet her there to make sure the staff was comfortable with the visit. Hospital visiting hours officially ended at 8:00 PM, but parents could visit their babies any time, day or night. Not that Mercy was a parent, but she was the closest thing that Lily's baby had.

"You'll have to scrub and put on a gown," the charge nurse said, eyeing Mercy with a scowl. Luckily, Mercy remembered the routine from her previous visit and she hoped this might win her a few points. "And I'll need to see some ID. Are you on the visitor list?" Mercy was so nervous that she dropped her purse, spilling the contents onto the floor as she searched for her wallet. She was almost in tears when she heard Barnes' familiar banter coming down the hall. His warm smile put her at ease and even the grumpy charge nurse softened when she saw him teasing Mercy.

"Thank God you're here," Mercy whispered. "That woman wanted to eat me alive!"

"She's alright," he said. "She's just a little protective of her babies."

This perspective was a welcome one and Mercy relaxed. Her focus shifted to the baby, who was sleeping peacefully despite the constant commotion all around him. She watched his chest rise and fall, finding comfort in the rhythm of his breathing. Again, she was struck by the lack of personal touch, compared to the areas surrounding the other babies. The only color at all was a blue teddy bear sticker on the index card taped to the isolette that read "Baby Boy" instead of a first name. Barnes seemed to read her thoughts. "This place could use a little cheering up," he said. "Maybe I'll bring the little guy his first football."

Mercy laughed. "Not exactly what I had in mind, but it would be an improvement."

Another nurse came in and looked at the baby's chart, hanging on the wall. She glanced up at Mercy and smiled. "You must be Auntie!" For a brief moment, Mercy was stunned. She had not really thought of herself as an aunt and it sounded funny. She had aunts, but they were old! This was going to take some getting used to. "Aunt Mercy," Barnes teased, smirking at her. She tried to hide the discomfort she was feeling at being addressed this way.

The nurse didn't seem to notice. Instead, she carefully explained everything she was doing, showing Mercy where she logged information, called vital signs, on the chart. "Everything is measured," she said, "how much formula he gets at every feeding and how wet each diaper is." The nurse checked his breathing, to make sure he was getting enough oxygen. "Most of his vitals are being monitored and recorded by all these electronics," she said, "but we don't like to rely solely on machines."

Mercy wanted to show that she was interested, but didn't really know how. "When does he eat?" she asked, hoping she didn't sound as dumb as she felt.

"Every two to three hours. We are trying our best to fatten him up," the nurse winked. "If you are here when it's time, I'll show you and even let you have a turn."

This pleased Mercy, even though it terrified her, at the same time. She had no experience at all with babies and feared she'd do it wrong. "Don't look so scared," Barnes said, once again displaying his police officer instincts and reading her mind. "If I can do it anybody can!"

Mercy was surprised. "You feed the babies?" she asked Barnes.

"Not here," he said, "but I feed *my* baby! I have a little guy at home, but he's a bigger model than this one." Barnes nodded toward Lily's baby. "Mine is almost two and a holy terror!" he said, with a hint of pride.

Mercy had not really thought of him as anything other than a police officer and she didn't know what to say. Barnes suddenly seemed a little embarrassed and saved her the trouble of responding. "Time for me to be getting home. Come on I'll walk you out."

She thanked the nurse and whispered good-bye to the baby, wishing suddenly that he had a name. But, first things first. Mercy secretly vowed to herself that she would try to buy him a stuffed toy.

Outside, Mercy used her cell phone to call the program. Staff had agreed to pick her up, since it was late and dark. Barnes waited with her for a few minutes, shuffling from foot to foot and glancing around the parking lot. "You know, Aunt Mercy, this is a good thing you are doing. Your sister may not appreciate it, but that little baby really needs someone to love him." Mercy thought she might cry, despite the aunt reference. All at once, she felt overwhelmed. But Barnes just smiled. "See you Saturday." He turned and headed across the lot, to his car. Mercy watched him walk away and thought about him going home to his little boy. She had noticed that he wore a wedding ring, but it never registered that Barnes was anything more than a cop. She wondered again if she was in over her head with this whole baby thing. But, Mercy was glad that at least Officer Barnes was on her side.

Chapter 16 Guilty Until Proven Innocent

Friday rolled around and Mercy was really looking forward to her next shift at the hospital, on Saturday morning. She rushed home from work and was deep in thought as the bus left her at the curb. She didn't see the police car in the driveway until she was about to open the front door of the program. Mercy's stomach reeled. She quickly entered the house, first passing the living room, where she glanced in. Some of the residents were gathered there, whispering feverishly. She headed straight back to the kitchen, where she was greeted by Kate, who looked somber, and Jess, who looked up but did not meet Mercy's eyes. Two police officers stood off to the side, one leaning on the counter, scribbling in a little black notebook. Before anyone could speak, Kate grimly announced, "This is Jess' roommate." Mercy froze.

The officer who was not writing gestured toward the program director's office and Mercy followed the silent direction. He was right behind her and closed the door, pointing to a chair. Mercy sat. He took the chair opposite her and looked at Mercy, his face blank of emotion. Mercy felt like time was moving very slowly. Finally, he spoke. "You know why I'm here." It was more of a statement than a question. Mercy managed a nod. "I have enough to arrest you right here and now," he continued, "but first I need to read you your rights."

"Arrest *me*?" Mercy found her voice. "But...why?"

"Larceny, for starters," he said. "Your roommate told us all about your little escapades at the mall, where I understand you are employed. Or maybe I should say, where you used to be employed. I can't imagine that your boss will be pleased to know you've been robbing the place blind on your lunch hour."

Mercy shook her head, to clear it. "But I didn't! I wouldn't!" It sounded lame, but Mercy didn't know what else to say. She was desperate to make him understand, but could not find the words.

"The evidence speaks for itself," the officer was saying, with a sneer. "We have the jewelry and the DVDs, from your closet. And, you're on probation, correct?" He raised his eyebrows.

Mercy's heart was hammering in her ears and she felt like she was sinking—fast. Just like in the movies, her life seemed to flash before her eyes. Mercy heard her mother's voice, saying, "All cops are pigs!" She thought about Lily, in her footed pajamas the night they were first taken away from their mother. She had a vision of Lily's baby, that first time she saw him and freaked out, running into the night. She thought about the stern face of the judge, banging his gavel in court as she struggled to understand her fate. Finally, she saw her sparse little desk and telephone, at work. Mercy knew that she had to stop this now. If she went to jail again, she would lose everything. And, as sad and pathetic as it might be, it was her life and she had worked hard to get where she was. And now, even Kate didn't believe her. Without plan-ning it, Mercy was standing and shouting. "I did not steal those things. I don't care what Jess told you because she is lying. And I can prove it."

The officer sat up straight and held up his hands, palms out. "Don't get excited. You have my attention. Why don't you sit back down and tell me how you are going to prove that you are innocent."

Back in the chair, Mercy took a deep breath. She started at the beginning, again, describing the scene on the day Jess arrived at the program. She told him how she later found the stolen items in the closet in Jess' closet. Finally, Mercy recounted her last session with her counselor. When she mentioned that she had written it all down and given it to Leslie, the officer raised his eyebrows once more, but reached for his note pad. After recording the therapist's name, address and phone number, he excused himself, directing Mercy to "stay put."

The office had a glass panel and Mercy could see the two patrolmen conferring in the hallway, their words too soft to comprehend through the closed door. The one who had interviewed Mercy was gesturing toward her and tapping the notepad with his pen. Then, he headed out the front door, but not before flashing Mercy a hostile glare. The first officer opened the door. "My partner is going to make some calls and try to check out your story," he said. "I'll need you back in the kitchen while we wait."

Jess and Kate were talking in hushed voices, but stopped abruptly when he led Mercy back into the room. Mercy searched Kate's face for some sign of support, but Kate only looked worried. Jess crossed her arms in front of her chest and slouched in the chair, turning away from Mercy. No one spoke. After several minutes of awkward silence, Kate excused herself. She returned a few moments later with a pizza box. "Anybody hungry?" she tried, with forced lightness. No one was. Mercy figured that the impromptu pizza party was the result of her being held hostage in the kitchen. She tried to smile at Kate, in apology. Kate just shrugged her shoulders and the quiet resumed.

The other officer sauntered back into the room, "It's our lucky day!" he said, still sounding skeptical. "The counseling agency closed at five, but the answering service reached your therapist," he said to Mercy. "She is on her way back to her office, but she needs your permission to talk to us." He directed his next comments to Kate, asking for the program's fax number to facilitate the exchange of information. Jess just stared straight ahead, clenching her jaw.

Kate led him back into the office, where the fax machine was located. Mercy said a silent prayer that Leslie would come through for her and that the police would see that Jess was lying. Looking over at her roommate, Mercy felt her anger soften, replaced by a deep sadness. Jess was pathetic, a victim of her own circumstances and too stubborn to even realize what she was doing. In the beginning, Mercy tried to be nice. She understood now that Jess was simply not capable of accepting her friendship.

Ten long minutes passed and the other officer emerged with a faxed document, placing it in front of Mercy, with a pen. "I'll need you to sign this to give Leslie your permission to share her records."

Mercy had seen such a paper before, when she gave Leslie permission to get her records from Child Services. She signed her name and filled in the date. The officer snatched it up without another word and disappeared again.

Eventually, he returned, with Kate in tow, and signaled the first officer back into the hallway. Jess shifted in her chair and gave a harrumph, as if she were the only one being inconvenienced at the moment. Kate looked at Mercy, warmth returning to her expression. Mercy took this as a good sign.

Abruptly, the two uniforms reappeared in the kitchen, all serious and business-like. The one who had called and faxed Leslie walked over to Jess and ordered her to stand. Mercy watched in horror as her roommate was placed in handcuffs. The officer recited the Miranda warning, like on television, and marched her out the back door. Jess was obviously embracing her right to remain silent, as she only stared at her own feet, still looking angry. The first police officer approached Mercy and she panicked, thinking she was next. But instead, he said, "Your story panned out. We're taking the letter you wrote with the counselor into evidence. We'll be in touch." He thanked Kate for her assistance and left. The flashing lights on top of the cruiser were reflected on the kitchen ceiling as the car left the program and merged into traffic. For Mercy, time had stretched like an elastic since she walked through the program's front door an hour earlier. All of a sudden, it snapped back and she became hypersensitive to her surroundings. The telephone was ringing and the other residents were outside the kitchen door, everyone talking at once, buzzing with excitement. Mercy collapsed into a chair, put her head on the table, and sobbed.

Chapter 17 Loyalty, Priorities, and Pizza

For several minutes, nobody bothered Mercy. She cried until her eyes burned and she had the hiccups. She felt a hand on her shoulder and raised her head to find Kate seated beside her at the kitchen table. The program was quiet again and they were alone. Kate slid a box of tissues toward her and Mercy pulled one out, wiping her nose. "Why didn't you come to me?" Kate asked. "We could have sorted it all out and then called the police ourselves."

"But how did they find out?" Mercy asked, sniffling.

"Staff went looking for Jess because she missed an appointment with her lawyer. The door was locked, so they entered, using a key. Jess was sitting on the bed, stuffing the things into a bag. She said that she had just found it all in your closet. So, we called the police. You're lucky you came home when you did, because they were going to arrest you at work!"

Mercy put her head back down on her folded arms and cried. "I'm sorry," she blubbered, "I just didn't know what to do and didn't want to get Jess in any more trouble."

Kate sighed. "Look at me, Mercy." Mercy lifted her head and turned her face to Kate. "You did the right thing by telling someone you trust," Kate continued. "But, in the future, you can always come to me—you *should* come to me—if it concerns what goes on in this house."

All she could manage was a nod, but Mercy was slowly beginning to feel better and a little relieved. She gave her nose a final blow. All at once, she was as exhausted as she'd ever been.

"I'll leave you in peace," Kate said, "But don't expect it to last long. The other residents are all worked up and you have quite a few phone messages to deal with."

She grabbed a glass of water and checked her messages. Mercy's social worker had called and she guessed that the program must have alerted her about the incident. Great, thought Mercy, she's probably home right now, adding a million new tasks to my service plan. That message could wait. Leslie had called, too, probably worried about how things turned out. Mercy returned her call, assuring her therapist that she was not in jail and that the police had believed her after reading the letter Mercy wrote a few days earlier.

Climbing the stairs took all the energy she had left. But seeing Jess' belongings in the room they shared unnerved her. She tried not to look at it as she showered and got ready for bed, but Jess seemed to be everywhere and Mercy began to feel badly again. Two of the other residents came by to see her. One offered support and brought some leftover pizza, while the other just wanted to gossip and pump her for information. When they finally left her alone again, Mercy looked ahead to tomorrow. She was going back to the hospital for another shift and a visit to Lily's baby. She groaned aloud when she remembered Barnes and realized that she would have to face him after he would, no doubt, hear all about the fiasco at the police station. As much as she wanted to put the situation behind her, Mercy had the feeling that it was only just beginning.

As she lay in bed that night, Mercy thought about Jess and what a mess she had made of everything. Still, she couldn't seem to muster the emotion to be angry with her roommate. Instead, Mercy was angry at herself for not handling things differently and for not making things turn out better. This feeling was not unfamiliar to her and Mercy's thoughts gradually turned to her sister. A few moments passed. Mercy sat up in bed with a start. "Lily!" she whispered to the empty room. Jess reminded her so much of Lily! Always starting over without really changing herself on the inside.

Mercy had tried to help them both and failed miserably. In the process, she had almost messed up her own life, and more than once. Mercy felt as if a veil had been lifted and she was seeing her life clearly for the first time. She felt the stirrings of anger, toward Jess and also toward Lily. Mercy had given them both so many chances. All she got in return was left behind to clean up the messes they made. She felt used. How could I be so stupid? Mercy wondered.

Once more, she promised herself that things were going to change. She needed to stop trying to help people who did not want to be helped. She had to start putting her own life first. And maybe that of Lily's baby. Who, by the way, needed a name. First thing Monday morning, she would call the baby's social worker to ask about that. Mercy realized that her stomach was growling because she had never eaten dinner. She threw back the covers and swung her legs over the edge of the narrow bed. All she could think about was that leftover pizza....

Chapter 18 *Unlikely Friends*

Saturday morning meant chaos at the hospital, especially in the ER. Mercy arrived for her shift and was immediately thrown into the mix. The hallway was lined with gurneys filled and patients waiting for a free examination room. Family members roamed about the area, leaving empty coffee cups and soda cans on every conceivable surface. Nurses were too frazzled to spend time finding something for her to do, so Mercy took a trash can from behind the main desk and started picking up the most obvious debris. Some of the patients were sleeping, but their family members were growing agitated and impatient. Many of them looked as if they had been there all night. Three hours went by before she knew it. Mercy slipped away to the cafeteria for an iced coffee. She took her time, stopping to look in the window at the hospital's small gift shop on the way back. A display of pink and blue roses, with matching teddy bears, reminded her that she'd be visiting Lily's baby again today. Mercy felt motivated to finish her shift and turned away from the window, heading back toward the ER. She collided with a tall figure coming out of the gift shop and looked up. It was Barnes. "Whoa! What's your hurry? Are you running from the police again?" Barnes elbowed her playfully.

Mercy ignored the jab. "If you must know, I am on my way back to work, which, by the way, is crazy busy. Where have you been all morning?"

"Funny you should ask." Barnes moved closer and glanced both ways, as if he were about to reveal a juicy bit of gossip. "I stopped at the station to drop off my paperwork for the week and ran into a fellow officer who was processing some evidence." Barnes lowered his voice to a whisper. "Seems there was some highly suspicious criminal activity at the shelter program last night. Was there something you should have told me, Mercy?"

Her heart sank and she looked away. The busy morning had provided a mental escape from last night's drama. Now, Mercy felt raw and exposed. Barnes was making light of it and it was far too soon for her to be joking about the incident. "I have to get back to work," she said, turning away. Tears stung her eyes and she walked quickly, willing him to stay behind. Barnes called after her, but Mercy ignored him. "We'll talk about this later," he called out, as she turned the corner.

She returned to the emergency room, where things seemed to be under control, at last. The morning shift of nurses and doctors increased the staff available to assist patients, all of whom had been moved to examination rooms. Mercy found only two new admissions. She helped them get settled, showing them where to store their clothing, helping them with the hospital gowns when necessary. Then she walked back to the nurse's station. The charge nurse thanked Mercy for her help, indicating that she was no longer needed. She headed to the elevators that would take her to the special care nursery.

There seemed to be more visitors on the weekend, Mercy thought. The nursery was buzzing with extra visitors, most babies having two parents and at least one grandparent tending to them. The bigger, stronger babies could be taken out of their cribs and rocked for short periods of time. Someday, maybe she'd be able to rock Lily's baby. For now, his little corner of the hospital was quiet, with only the beeping of his breathing and heart monitor. After performing the usual scrubbing routine and donning a gown, Mercy got comfortable on the high seat beside the baby's isolette. She placed her hands inside and gently stroked his tiny arms and legs. He was more alert today, opening his eyes, moving his limbs and even crying a little. The baby still appeared to be oblivious of her presence, but she remembered what the nurse had told her about the importance of being there and of touching him. Something about him always soothed Mercy and made it easier to let go of the rest of the world and her own problems. She stayed only thirty minutes, but it was long enough to comfort them both.

The bright sunshine blinded her when she reached the doors and entered the parking lot. It was just after noontime. She stepped off the curb, intent on starting toward the bus stop that would take her home to the program. "Mercy!" She turned around just as Barnes caught up to her, jogging up the sidewalk. "I was afraid I'd missed you. Couldn't let you leave mad at me. Are we still friends?" She rolled her eyes, unsure whether she was really ready to have this discussion. Barnes held out a small package. "I brought a peace offering," he said, smiling sheepishly. Mercy opened the bag and pulled out a small, blue teddy bear, like the ones she had seen in the hospital gift shop earlier right before she bumped into Barnes. "So that's what you were doing in there," she said, unable to stay angry. Mercy was touched by the thoughtful gesture and regretted running away from him outside the gift shop. The baby's little corner of the world could sure use this.

"Come back inside and let me buy you lunch," Barnes was saying. " I really do want to talk to you."

Her stomach was rumbling, so Mercy agreed. The distractions of a morning at the hospital and spending time with the baby had allowed her some distance from last night's events and the teddy bear softened her.

They went through the cafeteria line, choosing sandwiches and more iced coffee. Mercy followed Barnes to a small table in the corner, where they could talk somewhat privately. He looked up at her with no hint of a smirk this time. "I'm sorry about teasing you earlier. Are you alright, Mercy?"

She nodded, taking another bite of her lunch, and Barnes continued. "When I heard about the arrest at the program, I asked about you, naturally, and heard the whole story from the officers at the scene. It all worked out okay, but why didn't you come to me, Mercy? You almost ended up back in jail for the night!"

She swallowed. "I know. I know I screwed up. But I thought I was doing the right thing. I didn't really know what to do, so I went to see my counselor and told her everything. She had me write it all down and leave it with her. Thank God, they believed her." Mercy paused. "What about my roommate? What's going to happen to her?"

"She was waiting to go before a judge this morning," he said. "You won't have to share a room with her again, will you?"

Mercy thought about Jess' belongings all over her room and shuddered. "She can't come back to the program because this is at least her second arrest."

"Good!" Barnes said, sounding relieved. "You've given me enough gray hairs as it is. By the way, my wife put together a bag of things for the baby— just some things that we no longer need, like blankets and a couple of undershirts. I left them in the nursery when I went looking for you, but you'd already left."

Mercy was moved. She had planned to get some personal things for the baby something other than dingy hospital white. But the drama at the program had prevented her from even thinking about it. Barnes had come through, again.

After they said their good-byes, she couldn't resist going back to the nursery to see the baby one more time. She entered the area, which was still crowded with visitors. Lily's baby was wearing a tee shirt with little blue sailboats on it! She positioned the teddy bear on top of his unit, so that it sat facing anyone who came in to see him. She stood for a moment, memorizing his tiny face, admiring his new shirt. And Mercy smiled for the first time all day.

Chapter 19 *Feeling Transparent*

Mercy searched the food court for the familiar face, unsure she would even recognize her probation officer. She hadn't seen him since her court hearing and certainly didn't recognize his voice when he called earlier to suggest the meeting. For once, she was grateful for her short, forty-five-minute lunch break. At least she wouldn't have to endure it for long. She spotted him across the way, seated at a corner table, wearing a dark suit and staring at an open folder. *Oh God*, she thought, *could he look any more legit?* Mercy approached the small table and pulled out the chair opposite the PO. Her embarrassment continued when she glanced down and saw her name written on the tab of the folder he was reading. By the time he looked up, Mercy was already seated. He raised his eyebrows in greeting and looked her up and down, without smiling. Mercy started to sweat.

"How's it going, Mercedes?"

She was so stunned by his use of her real name that Mercy couldn't speak. She struggled to stifle the urge to laugh, knowing instinctively that it was not the appropriate response. She must have smirked, despite herself.

"Is something funny?" the PO asked, looking slightly annoyed.

"Sorry," Mercy stammered. "I'm not used to hearing my name. Everybody calls me Mercy. And it's going well, thank you."

"Let's go through the terms of your probation and see." He picked up a piece of paper and adjusted his glasses. "The program reports that you've made curfew every night. And your employer told me that you've made up any time you've taken off. I left a message for your therapist. Is she going to tell me you've kept all appointments?" He peered at Mercy over his glasses.

He didn't know her well enough to use the right name, but he knew everything about her. Mercy wrapped her sweater tightly around herself. She felt naked. "I see Leslie every two weeks," she told him. "And I have been doing my community service at the hospital, twice a week." She hoped she sounded confident and not angry, which was how she was beginning to feel. The PO didn't seem to notice. He skimmed down the page he was still holding. "Who's the contact person at the hospital?"

"Officer Mike Barnes supervises me and you can find him at the police department," Mercy said.

The probation officer looked up at her with a wrinkled forehead and nodded slowly. Finally, he seemed impressed. Mercy started to relax. "And your restitution fees are being paid on schedule," he added, closing the folder. "You make my job easy."

Mercy thought he sounded disappointed and guessed that he enjoyed being a jerk to anyone who did not follow the rules. "Well, I hardly have time to get into trouble between work, community service, and counseling. I basically have no life."

He smiled, at last. "That's the whole point." He stood, indicating that the meeting was over. Mercy was glad. At least she still had time to eat her lunch.

But she thought about it all afternoon and couldn't shake the feeling that the probation officer didn't really see her. She was only a file folder or a case number. He was so involved in her life, talking to everyone who knew her. She would definitely have gotten more of his attention if she had failed to follow the terms of her probation. Mercy thought about her mother. Probation officers were always a part of her life just like lawyers, police officers, and social workers. Her mother was always fighting with them, complaining about them, or hiding from them. If just one of them had actually bothered to know her, maybe things would have turned out differently for her mother and for Lily.

Mercy was reminded that she had intended to call the social worker for Lily's baby. As soon as she got home, she dialed the main number for Child Services and asked the receptionist to look up the social worker's name. Her call was put through, but he was not in, so Mercy left a message.

That night, Mercy allowed herself the fantasy that she would be able to choose a name for the baby. She had no idea where or how to begin. But she knew it would be a name that had meaning something that suited him. Her own name served as a good example of what *not* to do, she thought. Her mother had named her after something luxurious, something far removed from her own, miserable life. Maybe she thought it made her sound rich. Mercy snickered at the irony. No, Lily's baby would have a strong name. And, he would not be named after an automobile.

Chapter 20 Broken Promises

Mercy rode the escalator down to the ground level of the mall. She was on her way to the bookstore, where she hoped to buy something that might help her choose a name for Lily's baby. After thumbing through several editions, however, she was overwhelmed. *Did people actually pick names like this?* she thought. Some were hard to pronounce and would be impossible for a child to spell. Many of the names were feminine or too old-fashioned. Finally, she settled on a slim volume that seemed to have more traditional names.

For the rest of the afternoon, Mercy was distracted and glanced at the book whenever she had a free minute. The baby's social worker had not returned her call. But Mercy knew that she needed to call him something other than "Baby Boy," which was still written on his hospital chart and on his isolette. During her last visit, one of the other mothers on the unit asked, "What's your baby's name?" Mercy felt so foolish when she replied, "I don't know—I mean he doesn't have one yet." The woman looked surprised, as she smiled and walked away. Next time, Mercy would be prepared.

Her own social worker stopped by the program that evening, just as Mercy arrived home from work. She asked about the meeting with probation and Mercy filled her in. "He's not exactly warm and fuzzy."

"He's okay," her worker said. "And he's got bigger fish to fry than you. Just keep doing everything he asks and you won't even be on his radar. What else is going on?"

Mercy told her about the call to the baby's social worker. "Usually, in a case like that, the foster parents suggest a name," she replied, "especially if they want to adopt him. But Lily's baby is a long way from being ready to leave the hospital, so no foster family has been identified yet."

Mercy's heart sank at the thought of the baby no longer being at the hospital, where she could see him. "But I'm his family!" she blurted. "What about me?"

"Well, if you are serious about being in the baby's life, we'll have to have a conversation with his social worker. There will be a lot of work to be done, Mercy. For starters, you need to be off probation and have a place to live that will accommodate a baby." Disappointment was obvious on Mercy's face. "Let's not get ahead of ourselves. Why don't you start by talking with the baby's social worker about a name and make sure he knows that you are involved. I'll try to follow up with him when I get to the office in the morning."

Mercy barely touched her dinner that night. She was too preoccupied with the overwhelming tasks before her. She already had too much to do and now, there were even bigger things to worry about. How would she ever manage it? She decided to skip movie night at the program and headed upstairs to her room. When she saw the book of baby names on the bed, Mercy nearly burst into tears. She felt silly for being so excited about picking a name, when there were so many more important issues looming. She flung herself on the bed. Mercy closed her eyes and remembered....

Lily was about five and two years younger than Mercy, but she had not started school yet. They were on an overnight visit with their mother because she had been to the hospital and had stopped drinking. The school bus was supposed to pick Mercy up in the morning. But her mother hadn't woken her. Mercy had gotten some cereal for Lily and put her in front of the television. Then, she dressed herself in the same clothes that she had worn the day before. When she went to her mother's room, Mercy turned on the light. Her mother was not in bed. Mercy called out for her.

She looked in the bathroom and even in the closet. Lily came to see what she was yelling about, carrying her breakfast. She spilled her cereal and started to cry. Mercy heard the school bus outside, blowing the horn. She couldn't leave Lily alone. After a minute, she heard the bus drive away. Mercy made sure the door was locked. She knew her mother would get in trouble if anyone found they were alone. She got Lily some more cereal and poured some for herself. There was no more milk so Mercy ate hers dry. Then she cleaned up the dishes and reminded Lily to go potty. Mercy got some clothes for Lily and dressed her sister, but she couldn't tie her shoes, so she let her go barefoot, not wanting her to slip in her stocking feet.

Eventually, Lily wanted her mother and started to cry. She cried so hard that she had the hiccups. Mercy tried to make her drink some water, but Lily vomited all over herself. Then, somebody was knocking at the door and calling her mother's name. Mercy calmed her little sister down and they hid behind the couch, where nobody could see them. But whoever was at the door did not go away. Instead, there were soon sirens and lights flashing in the driveway. The front door burst open and a policeman came in, calling their names, followed by a social worker. They asked Mercy a lot of questions, about when she last saw her mother and where her mother might have gone. The social worker cleaned Lily up and hurriedly put both girls in her car. Mercy heard her mother's voice before she actually saw her. She was screaming at the social worker to stop, but the police officer held her, keeping her from reaching them. He waved the social worker on and the car started to move, away from their home, away from their mother. The last thing she heard her mother shout was, "Take care of your sister!"

Mercy shook off the memory and picked up the book of baby names. Maybe I didn't take care of my sister, she thought, but I will take care of her baby.

Chapter 21 *What's in a Name?*

Mercy stayed up late reading through the book of baby names. She found a few that she liked right away and looked further to see what traits they inspired in those who bore the names. She was so determined that Lily's baby would have a fitting name that she decided to sleep on it. But the one name she most favored supposedly meant that he would love the security of a stable home and family, be easy going and charming, as well as understanding, confident and successful. Mercy couldn't think of anything better to wish for.

When she got to work the next day, she checked her cell phone and found a voicemail from the baby's social worker. She hit the call back button and took a deep breath. He answered on the first ring. She launched into a rehearsed speech about her wanting to be a part of her sister's baby's life, being the only family he has. Then, Mercy brought up the issue of naming him. "That seems a reasonable request," the social worker replied, "but understand that it might be temporary. I can't guarantee the name will stick once he is placed in a foster home." Mercy swallowed her fears and forged on. "I talked with my social worker about it," she continued, trying to sound important. "I want to be able to take care of the baby, when he is ready." Mercy could hear her own heart beating in the short silence that followed.

"Let's set up a meeting," he said. "Maybe your social worker can join us and we can look at your options. But in the meantime, what did you have in mind for a name?"

"Timothy," she said, liking it even as it rolled off her tongue. "That's a good name," the social worker said. "I think we can all live with that, at least for now."

Mercy ended the call and could not suppress a big smile. He hadn't said no. He wanted to meet her and he liked the name. She was thrilled and terrified, all at the same time. She hoped the day wouldn't drag—she was scheduled to volunteer at the hospital after work and could hardly wait to see the baby—to see Timmy.

At five o'clock, Mercy headed to the hospital. Her shift in the emergency room went by quickly, as usual. There was a steady flow of patients and concerned family members who required her assistance. Officer Barnes was working security and had to guard a noisy patient who was uncooperative. Mercy brought him a sandwich from the cafeteria when she took a break, but he was still tied up when her shift ended and she headed upstairs to the nursery.

She was happy to see the baby was wearing another of the hand-me-down undershirts, this one with little blue stripes. He was sleeping on his back while the monitors clicked a soothing rhythm. Mercy reached into her pocketbook and pulled out a blue marker. She removed the ID card from the isolette. In the space where a nurse had printed "Baby Boy," Mercy printed "Timothy" in big, dark letters. She replaced the card and smiled with approval. The baby stirred and opened his eyes. "Hello, Timmy," Mercy whispered. She placed her hands inside and stroked his arms and legs. He returned to his sleepy state. "I guess you're not impressed," she said, chuckling.

The unit was quiet and Mercy looked around, hoping another baby's family might speak to her. She was anxious to use the new name, to try it out again. But the other visitors were absorbed in their own babies. Eventually, one of the nurses came in and she noticed the new name right away. "That's a good, strong name for a boy," she said. "Is it official? I can change it in the computers, if it is." As much as Mercy wanted to say yes, she did not want to get into trouble with the social worker, so she suggested the nurse check with him first. But she was secretly thrilled when the nurse called him by name during her quick check of his vital signs and monitor.

Before she left, Mercy took out her phone and snapped a photo of the sleeping baby. She made it her wallpaper before returning the phone to her bag. With every visit, it was getting harder to leave him. Maybe having his picture to look at would help.

On the bus ride home, Mercy took the phone out and looked at the photo again. She wished she had someone to share it with. In a rare moment, she missed her mother and her sister. Before now, they were the only family she knew. There had been some nice foster parents along the way and a few foster siblings. But she had not loved them. They were not the same as a real family. Mercy silently promised to be a real family for Timothy.

Chapter 22 *A New Plan*

Mercy was early for her counseling appointment with Leslie. In the waiting room, she tried to organize her thoughts, but her emotions were all over the place. She hoped that her therapist could help her focus on what needed to be done. The meeting with her social worker and Timmy's was scheduled for later in the week. Mercy was excited and very overwhelmed. She did not want to blow it. The facts were stacked against her, she knew, but yet, there was something driving her forward.

Leslie was her usual calm and neutral self as Mercy described the events of the past week, including her conversations with the two social workers from Child Services. "How much longer is your probation?" Leslie asked. "That seems like the first and most obvious obstacle."

Mercy knew she was right. The judge would never approve an eighteen-year-old on probation as a suitable placement for a new baby. "My court review is next month," she said, "but there is no way my restitution will be paid off by then. I have a few hundred dollars in the bank, but I am going to need that, if I am going to find an apartment."

"Housing is going to be a big issue, too," Leslie said. "Rents are expensive and require first, last, and security deposit, up front."

Mercy's shoulders sagged and she stared at her hands in her lap. "I need to come up with a plan before that meeting, or Timmy is going to a foster home who will adopt him and I won't stand a chance."

Leslie softened. "Well, I don't work for the state, but it seems to me that you have one thing going for you that no foster parent ever will—you are Timothy's family. You are blood and that has to count for something. Let's look at the next thirty days and see what you can accomplish. That way, you will go into court prepared."

Mercy brightened. "My terms of probation are all being met. But I am so busy, between that, the hospital and work I cannot imagine adding anything else."

"Word of advice," Leslie said. "Being a parent, especially to a baby, is not easy, so complaining about having too much to do will *not* help your case."

"I just don't know what to do first," Mercy said. "I've never had a baby before!"

"That might be a good place to start, actually. If you had given birth to a baby like Timothy, what would Child Services be asking you to do?"

Mercy chewed her bottom lip. "Maybe I can ask my social worker? I can call her later."

"Good thinking, Mercy. I think you need to take the initiative rather than waiting for them to tell you what to do. Don't be afraid to be your own advocate."

She liked the sound of that. And she liked having a task that she could do, rather than feeling overwhelmed. Mercy agreed to meet with Leslie again in two weeks to talk about her progress and develop a more specific plan.

As soon as she got to work, she called her social worker, who was in a meeting. When she called back an hour later, Mercy asked what she would have to do if she had a baby of her own. The social worker was startled and misinterpreted the request. Mercy had to explain that she wanted to start preparing to take care of her sister's baby. Once she recovered, the social worker was helpful. "Off the top of my head, I would say parenting classes. We'd also look at your support system, like extended family that is available to help. I know that's a hard one for you, Mercy. If I think of anything else, I will let you know at our meeting later this week."

But she gave her the numbers for two agencies that offered parenting classes. On her break, Mercy called them. The first had a long waiting list. She had better luck with the second, but the classes were during the day. Leslie's words came back to her she was right. This was not going to be easy. Her schedule was already full and she could not take time off because she was going to need the money. She decided to ask her boss about changing her schedule. Maybe she could take the hour off and make it up during the evening. She sent an email asking to speak with him, before she lost her nerve.

When she returned from lunch, he was waiting by her desk, looking concerned. "Is everything alright, Mercy?"

She blushed, uncomfortable with the attention. For the past year, she had come and gone without engaging with anyone any more than was absolutely necessary. Now, she had to reveal her most personal information. Mercy started to regret the move as she followed him into his office and he closed the door. He smiled and suggested she take a seat. Taking a deep breath, Mercy explained about her sister having a baby and running away. Her boss looked surprised, but nodded encouragement as she spoke. When she finished, he waited a moment before speaking. "I'm sorry, Mercy. I had no idea you were going through this. Of course we'll help. The mall has policies and there are laws about family leave. And you're only asking for an hour. We will pay you for the time it will take for parenting classes, and we'll talk about any court time you need to take off, when the time comes."

Mercy was dumbfounded. She had no idea that she was entitled to time off to take care of these things. She felt a burden lift from her shoulders as the first piece of a huge puzzle fell into place. She thanked her boss, awkwardly but profusely, fighting the urge to jump for joy as he handed her the required paperwork for her time off. She called the agency back and scheduled to begin parenting instruction the following Monday at 9:00 AM. Before closing her phone, she glanced at the photo of Timmy that still served as her wallpaper. Mercy smiled and she made a mark beside one more thing on her mental checklist.

Chapter 23 *The Folder*

The next day was Friday and Mercy woke early. This was the day. She lay in bed, thinking about the meeting with her social worker and Timmy's. She knew what she wanted to say, but she was nervous that it wouldn't come out right or that they would shut her down because they still viewed her as a kid herself. She decided to put her thoughts on paper, to help her focus and make sure she didn't forget anything important. Grabbing a notebook and pen, Mercy slipped into her bathrobe and headed downstairs. She was going to need a cup of coffee to fortify herself.

The program was still quiet and she was surprised to find Kate in the kitchen so early. "What are you doing up so early?" Kate asked, clearly as surprised as Mercy.

She plopped down and held up the notebook. "Trying to make some notes," Mercy said, rolling her eyes hopelessly. "I am meeting with the social workers today, to talk about Timmy and where he is going to live when he is ready to leave the hospital."

"Oh, wow," Kate said, "are you going to ask them to let him live with you?"

Mercy nodded, realizing how ridiculous the idea sounded when put so bluntly. She stared at the blank page in her notebook. "I wish I knew where to start."

Kate brought her a cup of coffee and sat down across from Mercy at the kitchen table. "You know that you can't live here with a baby." It was more a question than a statement and Mercy nodded again, beginning to feel miserable. "But," Kate continued, "the agency has a sister program across town that is designed for young parents with newborns."

Mercy's head shot up and she met Kate's eyes. "What?!" She was afraid she had heard it wrong.

"There are eight units and each has a teen mother and her baby living in it. They provide childcare classes and daycare while the moms finish school, and other support, like we do here, but geared toward parenting."

Mercy's heart skipped a beat, or maybe two. Maybe there was something like this for her, where she could care for Timmy and the social workers would still be involved. She could have Timmy *and* her program. Picking up her pen, Mercy started writing her list. She was so engrossed in the task that she didn't hear Kate leave the room. When she returned, she dropped a folder on the table next to Mercy. "Put your notes in here," Kate said, "and you will look like a professional."

Mercy showered and dried her hair quickly. Standing in front of her meager closet, she struggled with what to wear. Most of her work outfits were pretty casual, but she settled on black pull-on pants and a plain sweater. She wished she had some decent jewelry or knew how to wear a scarf, like she had seen other women do. Her social worker always lectured her about dressing nicely for court instead of looking like a rock star, so Mercy figured that would help. She tucked the folder under her arm and headed for the bus stop.

Mercy sat in the waiting room at the Department of Child Services and looked around. She had been here so many times in her life, but this was the first time she had sat alone, waiting to be called in for a meeting. Usually, her social worker would have picked her up in her car and brought her straight back to her desk, where she would have a snack while waiting. Mercy crossed her legs and looked down at the folder on her lap. She really did feel like a grown-up. Eventually, her social worker entered the lobby and led Mercy to a small conference room, where Timmy's social worker was waiting.

He stood and shook her hand, which Mercy liked and took as a good sign, even though he appeared serious and business-like.

Each social worker opened a manila folder and placed a pen beside it. Mercy silently thanked Kate for providing her with a folder this morning, noting that hers was much nicer than theirs. Timmy's worker began. "I have read through some of your record," he said. "I know that you're at the Independent Living program and working at the mall. I also know that you are on probation." He looked up from his notes. "Why don't you tell me what else is going on and what makes you a good resource for the baby."

Taking a deep breath, Mercy began. "Well, I visit him at the hospital twice a week. The nurse said she would show me how to feed Timmy as soon as he is able to be held outside the isolette for longer periods of time. And I will be starting parenting classes on Monday."

"Okay," he said, drawing out the second syllable. "When will your probation be over?"

"I am doing all of the things they've asked and have a court appearance in four weeks," Mercy said. "But my court fines won't be paid off for another three months."

"And what about the charges?" he asked.

Mercy's social worker chimed in. "The charges are continued without a finding and will be dismissed if she complies with the terms of probation and pays the restitution in full." Mercy still wasn't sure what all that meant, but she thought it sounded good.

She opened her folder and looked at her notes. *So far, so good*, she silently told herself. "I have a question about housing. I know that there is a program for teen mothers with babies? I'd like to know more about that."

Her social worker smiled. "You've done your homework, Mercy! There is a program like that, but it is usually reserved for moms who are still in highschool and have had a baby. I can look into it and see if they would accept a working mom—or, in your case, a working aunt. Both you and the baby are in state custody, so that should help. But the program is always full and it's really hard to find an opening." She turned to Timmy's worker. "What's the time frame for the baby? Do we know when he will be ready for discharge?"

There was a knot in Mercy's stomach, waiting for the answer. She needed time and she knew it was going to be close. He looked at his notes again before answering. "Looks like he will be there another month," he said, "barring any complications. I should be making a referral for a foster parent to be identified soon, so they can start going to the hospital and learning about the baby's care."

Mercy's heart sank and she tried hard to keep her composure. "I can ask the nurses to teach me everything there is to know," she said, perhaps a little too eagerly. She looked from one social worker to the other. They looked at each other. He shrugged. Her social worker said, "I can't see the harm in that, as long as the hospital is willing. Do you have anything else in that folder that you want to share, Mercy?"

"Just that I am willing to do whatever it takes to stay in Timmy's life. I am the only family he has and he is mine. I think that should count for something."

Chapter 24 *Seeing Things Differently*

The work day dragged after the meeting at Child Services, but it was finally five o'clock. She walked to the bus stop distractedly. But when she got there, Mercy kept walking. Impulsively, she decided to walk to the hospital for an unscheduled visit with Timmy. After all that had happened in the past couple of days, she just wanted to see him. She hoped one of the nicer nurses would be working, figuring they wouldn't mind that she was there without Officer Barnes.

She walked into the special care nursery and stopped short, thinking that she had accidentally entered the wrong room. The isolette was empty and a nurse was standing with her back to Mercy. She started to back out of the room, but the nurse turned to face her. She was holding Timmy! "You're just in time," she said. "I'm about to change and feed him."

Mercy plopped down in the rocking chair. The nurse smiled. "Well, you won't learn how to change him sitting on your bum." Mercy shot up from the rocker and followed her over to the high dresser where she placed the sleeping baby on his back. He was wrapped in a blanket and she peeled it off him, revealing his tiny arms and legs, as well as the small, round stickies where the electrical leads were pasted on his chest. She worked quickly but spoke softly to Timmy the whole time. Mercy was amazed, taking it all in.

"Next time, I'll let you change him," she said. Mercy could only nod in reply. "Why don't you feed him?" Mercy's fear and surprise must have showed on her face because the nurse smiled. "Don't worry you won't break him!"

After she washed her hands and put a hospital gown over her clothing, Mercy sat awkwardly in the rocking chair beside the isolette. The nurse gently placed the baby in her arms and she tried desperately to remember how she had seen others hold babies. He felt warm and more solid than she expected. The nurse handed her the bottle and showed Mercy how to hold it to his lips. Timmy latched on and sucked ferociously, making Mercy giggle. "See? There's nothing to it!" the nurse said. "He still has the connectors and is attached to the monitors, but they won't get in the way. I'll be right over there if you need me." She went across the room to tend to the other babies. Mercy thought she must be dreaming. She tried to relax her arms, which were beginning to cramp from holding Timmy so stiffly. She marveled at his small, delicate features and the strength of his jaws locked around the bottle's nipple. Soon, he seemed to drift off to sleep and the bottle floated loosely in his lips. Mercy knew she should put the bottle down and try to burp him, but she couldn't imagine how to do it without growing an extra set of hands. Just then, the nurse returned to check on her. "I think he's done," Mercy said tentatively. The nurse took the bottle from her and helped Mercy lift the baby to a sitting position on her lap, showing her how to support his head so that it wouldn't roll forward. She patted his back for a full minute, beginning to feel foolish with no results. Suddenly, Timmy burped loudly and Mercy laughed out loud, startled by the force of it.

"Good job!" the nurse said triumphantly. "I'll let you rock him for a few more minutes before he needs to be put back to bed."

Mercy sat with Timmy sleeping against her in the quiet room. All of the monitors were silent and she could hear his breathing for the first time. That same peacefulness that Mercy had felt the first time he curled his tiny fingers around hers returned. Instead of feeling nervous or overwhelmed, Mercy felt happy and confident. She wished the moment would last forever.

But the magic was broken by the nurse. She took Timmy from Mercy and her shoulder felt cold and empty in his absence. A small sadness began to swell inside her.

Once Timmy was back in his isolette, Mercy thanked the nurse and headed for the lobby. Tomorrow was Saturday. She would be back to do her usual shift of volunteer work and then she would see Timmy again. As she walked to the bus stop, her stomach began to growl and Mercy realized she had not eaten dinner. Hopefully, someone at the program had saved her a plate. She climbed aboard the bus and found a window seat, her thoughts returning to Timmy as the bus moved away from the curb. Mercy was excited that he was able to come out of the isolette and be free of the monitors for short periods of time. But she also knew that the clock was ticking for him to be discharged from the hospital. What if he went to a foster home and they decided to adopt him? The thought was almost too much to bear. Mercy simply could not imagine her life without Timmy in it.

Back at the program, she went through the motions, checking in with staff and finding some leftovers in the kitchen. The place she had come to call home seemed changed in some way—as if it was lacking something vital. Mercy felt uneasy, as if she had outgrown the place and no longer belonged there. She looked around at the plain walls and battered furniture. Things were the same as they had always been. Mercy realized that it was she who was different. The program had served a purpose in her life, but she needed more—she wanted more. Her life at the program suddenly felt like something from the past. Mercy recalled the social workers coming to tell her about Lily's baby. She thought about the day she had bolted from the hospital, fell asleep in the park and spent a night in jail. The night she met Mike Barnes. She remembered her roommate Jess and the police and the stolen jewelry. Then, she thought about today: how she had sat at the Child Services office with her nice folder and how she had spoken up at the meeting. She had fed Timmy a bottle and rocked him to sleep. Things were happening, but Mercy wished she had a fast-forward button. She wanted her probation to be over, her court fines to be paid, and to move into some place where she could live with Timmy. Her mind was racing. Tomorrow, she would have to do more. But for now, it was going to be a long night...

Chapter 25 *A Big Surprise*

Mercy was ten minutes early for her shift at the hospital emergency room. She checked in with the nursing supervisor and went about her usual routine of emptying waste baskets and directing family members to the cafeteria or restrooms. She had become familiar with the hospital and comfortable with her duties, which allowed her to think about Timmy while she worked. She hoped he might be ready to have a bottle again today when she finished her work. Mercy looked for Officer Barnes as she moved about, too. He had been busy the last few shifts and she hadn't had much opportunity to talk with him. She wanted to share the news about Timmy's progress. She didn't have many friends and certainly none who would understand about her sister's baby. Even though Barnes was older, he was a dad and he understood about Timmy. And he had seen Mercy at her lowest point and still tried to be her friend.

The charge nurse stopped Mercy as she passed by the nurses' station. "Would you mind covering for another volunteer, Mercy? She is sitting with a patient who came in alone—a drug overdose. But she needs to take a bathroom break. Just ring me if the patient wakes up." She headed down the corridor feeling a little anxious. Mercy had not had much direct contact with patients. The other volunteer promised to be back in ten minutes and Mercy sat on the hard chair beside the bed. A small form was still beneath the blankets, her back to Mercy. An IV pole on the other side of the bed delivered clear fluid while a monitor beeped intermittently and displayed blinking numbers. A patch of dirty blond hair was visible on the pillow. The patient began to stir and Mercy silently prayed she would not wake up. But when she struggled against the covers and rolled over, Mercy found herself looking straight into the eyes of her sister. Lily blinked but stared ahead, unseeing, before closing her eyes again. Mercy didn't move. She was holding her breath and slowly exhaled. This was not happening. This couldn't be Lily. Her eyes darted around the room, looking for clues. She saw the patient file hanging off the end of the bed. It was strictly against hospital policy for her to touch the medical record. But she wasn't thinking rationally. She wasn't really thinking at all. Mercy reached the foot of the bed with no memory of leaving her chair. Before she could reach for the file, she saw Lily's name printed across the binding, in big, black letters. Mercy fainted.

When she woke up, Mercy was being wheeled into a small space in the emergency room, divided by curtains on three sides. An orderly was pushing the gurney and he smiled. "She's awake!" he shouted out into the brightly-lit hallway. The doctor on duty appeared at her feet. "Can you remember what happened?" he asked. But she was confused and couldn't answer him. Somehow, she had ended up in this bed. But, how? "One of the other volunteers found you on the floor of the room where you were watching a patient," the doctor said.

Mercy gasped and tried to sit up as she remembered what happened. But the room started to spin and she was forced to fall back onto the pillow. "Lily," was all she could say. The doctor raised his eyebrows and pulled a small scope out of his breast pocket. He shined a light into one of Mercy's eyes and then the other, speaking as he worked. "So, who is Lily?"

"My sister," Mercy managed. "The patient I was watching. She's my sister." Mercy started to cry.

The doctor nodded as he began to understand what had happened. A nurse appeared and he spoke to her, but continued to look at Mercy. "She's had a bit of a shock. Let's keep her calm and let her get some rest, but she's going to be fine." He made some notes on a clipboard and left. The nurse stroked Mercy's arm and tried to soothe her. Another nurse appeared, carrying two paper cups, one with water and the other with a small pill that Mercy swallowed. Within minutes, she drifted off to sleep.

The next time she opened her eyes, Officer Barnes was standing beside the bed. His worried look was replaced by his usual grin when he saw that Mercy was awake. "Well, hello there, Sleeping Beauty," he said. "Some people will go to any length to avoid working." She tried to return his smile, but Mercy was still a bit disoriented. Barnes became serious again. "Lily is fine," he said. "She is getting some medicine to help her detox safely. But she's going to be okay."

Mercy nodded. "Does she know Timmy is here?"

Barnes shrugged. "I've told you all that I know. Once you're up and around, maybe you can see her yourself."

Mercy sat up, slowly this time. She swung her feet off the bed and looked around for her shoes. "Not so fast," Barnes said, "I think a nurse needs to check you out before you disappear."

As if on cue, a nurse appeared, accompanied by the hospital social worker—the same woman who had interviewed Mercy about the community service job. How embarrassing, she thought. But this time, she was more interested in Lily. Apparently, she was being less than forthcoming about her recent history. Hospital records showed that she was positive for cocaine and marijuana at the time of the baby's birth. Mercy explained that she had not had any contact with her sister since before Timmy's arrival. In fact, she had not even known Lily was pregnant until the baby was born. She told them that Lily had run from the hospital by the time Mercy arrived to see her and her baby. She desperately hoped that they did not make the connection between that evening and Mercy's own bolting from the hospital, followed by her eventual arrest. But the hospital social worker seemed satisfied and left the nurse to discharge Mercy, who was feeling more alert and almost like her old self again.

The nursing supervisor advised Mercy that her shift was officially over and that she was to go home and continue resting.

But, first, she had to see Lily.

Chapter 26 *Lily*

The elevator doors slid open and Mercy stepped out, searching the signs for the room number she had been given for Lily. An arrow pointed to the left, so she started down the shiny, bright-ly-lit corridor. The psych ward was locked and Mercy had to ring a bell and wait to be buzzed inside. According to the hospital social worker, Lily had eventually agreed to get help. But first, she had to detox for three days while an open bed was found at a drug treat-ment program. Mercy had been warned that her sister was not in a good frame of mind. She had been combative in the emergency room and was feeling sick as the drugs wore off. But nothing could have prepared Mercy for what happened next. As she neared the room, she could hear shouting and cursing. It sounded like furni-ture was being tossed around. Two nurses and an orderly ran past her, turning into Lily's room. They were followed closely by Barnes, who was acting in his role as a security guard.

Mercy approached the room and peered inside. A chair was tipped on its side and the privacy curtain surrounding the bed was torn and hanging from one hook. The bed was crooked, one end pushed against the windows. Her eyes found Lily, who was on the floor, arms and legs splayed out to the sides, and there was a nurse kneeling over her, holding her down. The yelling and swearing was coming from Lily, but she seemed to be running out of steam. For a minute, nobody noticed Mercy. A nurse was taking down the ripped curtain and the orderly was picking things up, including the chair. Barnes was squatting before Lily, at a safe distance, talking to her in a soothing but firm tone. Lily quieted somewhat and relaxed her flailing limbs. She dropped her face onto the bare floor and began to cry big, gulping sobs.

"Get off her!" Mercy screamed as she ran toward her sister. Barnes stood quickly and intercepted Mercy, wrapping her in a bear hug and leading her from the room. In the hallway, he released his hold, but gripped Mercy's wrist. "Let me go!" Mercy struggled against him. Barnes now talked to Mercy in the same comforting manner.

"They are not hurting her. Lily is being restrained to keep her safe." Barnes had to repeat the statement three times before the information registered and she calmed down. "Mercy, you probably shouldn't be here right now. Lily is in the throes of withdrawal and is going to need to get it out of her system before she can be rational. Why don't you go home? I'll call you at the end of my shift and let you know how she's doing."

Mercy let her arms go limp. She felt defeated and realized that he was right. Lily was in no shape to talk about Timmy. At least her sister was in a safe place. She knew nothing else really mattered right now, but she feared that Lily would run away again before she had a chance to see her. Barnes read her thoughts. "Lily's not going anywhere," he said. "She's on a locked ward and will be watched closely after that little fiasco. And she certainly will not be allowed visitors tonight."

Mercy was in the program's battered van and on her way home before she knew it. She looked over at Kate, who was driving. "How did you know what happened?" Mercy asked.

Kate smiled. "The hospital must have called Child Services because your social worker called and asked us to pick you up, once you were medically cleared. But what happened after that, Mercy?"

She told Kate the whole story, about seeing her sister being restrained by the nurse and then not being allowed to talk to Lily. "I don't even remember the last time I saw her," Mercy said. "It was such a shock!"

"Your sister sure is full of surprises, Mercy. But I guess that's not something you ever get used to. I'm sure you will get to see her tomorrow, when she is in better condition."

"I sure hope so," Mercy said, feeling doubtful again.

Later, she was sitting up in bed, her mind churning with questions that nobody could answer. She was holding her phone and looking at the picture she had taken of Timmy last week. Would Lily want to see him? Would she ever come to love him the way Mercy did? Just then, the phone buzzed and startled her. Mercy tapped the screen and a text message from Barnes appeared. "Lily is sleeping peacefully. No more trouble tonight. Hope you are sleeping, too." She turned the phone off and pulled up the covers. Mercy was in for another long night.

Chapter 27 *Finding Friends in Unusual Places*

Mercy rolled over and stretched, squinting against the sunlight streaming into her room. It was almost a full minute before she remembered the events of the previous day. Her sister was back! And she couldn't leave—at least not yet. Mercy jumped out of bed and dressed quickly. There was no time to waste.

She wasn't sure of the Sunday bus schedule, so Mercy decided to walk to the hospital. It was a nice day and she stopped only for an iced coffee, to fortify herself, along the way. The steady rhythm of her sneakers against the sidewalk provided background music that allowed her mind to wander. She imagined Lily going to rehab and staying this time, wondering what the grown-up version of her sister might be like. Lily was still her little sister, but she had lived on the streets, had a baby and done God knows what else. She was only sixteen, but her experiences had been very different than Mercy's. Somehow, she could not imagine Lily living in a program, going to work every day and meeting with a social worker. She had never been able to fit in with foster families or new schools. She got into trouble, broke the rules, and ran away. Was history about to repeat itself?

Mercy arrived at the hospital. It was beginning to feel like her second home. It was quieter than usual this morning and Mercy looked for familiar faces among the weekend staff. But nobody acknowledged her as she made her way to the elevators and the psych floor. A nurse she didn't recognize buzzed her through the doors. Mercy practically tiptoed to her sister's room and peeked in. Lily was sitting up in bed, staring out the window. "Lily?" Mercy asked, timidly. She turned her head and looked at Mercy for a long moment.

"Well. If it isn't Miss Goody Two-Shoes."

Mercy's heart sank. In her imagined reunion with Lily, she had not envisioned this. "How are you feeling?"

Lily harrumphed and crossed her arms in front of her chest. "I was fine until the hospital social worker came in this morning. She knew all about me and the baby and our miserable life. And, thanks to you, I cannot even see the baby until Child Services comes and asks me a million more stupid questions. Why can't you just butt out of my life for a change and mind your own business?!"

"But I didn't tell them anything—how could I? I haven't seen you in almost a year, Lily! Of course they know about the baby— he is still here! And you are still in state custody, so of course the social worker had to be told you were back."

"Why do you always take their side? You think you're so smart! Well, I have news for you I am going to stop you from taking the baby. He is mine, not yours, and don't you forget it."

Mercy fought back tears that burned her eyes. "You can't do that, Lily. I am all he has!"

"Not anymore. I'm back and he is my baby, so you'd better get used to it. And, for the record, his name is not Timmy. What gives you the right to name my baby? You can take your saint act some-where else. Maybe you should get a life, Mercy. Then you could get out of my life and stay out!"

Mercy ran from the room just as a nurse was coming in to see what the shouting was about. She held back the tears until she got to the lobby and out the main entrance. She ran into a small alcove at the corner of the building, where no one could see her. Mercy wailed. She doubled over and sobbed for a full minute, until she could no longer breathe and thought she might vomit. Then, she leaned against the building and the bricks felt cool against her back. What in the world am I going to do? she thought desper-ately. She couldn't lose Timmy. But Lily was his mother and she knew her sister would be given a chance. But what did that mean for Mercy?

She dried her eyes and gulped some big breaths. And then she started walking. Once again, Mercy knew, she needed a plan. But she was too distraught to think of one. She had always tried to do the right thing, to be the kid who played by the rules, even when they kept changing. But Lily always got the attention. She was always the trouble-maker. Mercy tried to help her sister, but she was beyond help. And then there was her roommate, Jess. Mercy had tried to help her, too, and look where that got her. Now, Mercy finally had something—someone she cared about. And he needed her. Damn Lily for showing up just in time to ruin it all! The angrier she felt, the faster she walked. By the time she reached the program, Mercy was steaming. She let the front door bang shut behind her.

Kate looked up as she passed the living room. "Hey, Mercy! Can you give me a hand with lunch today?"

"Why are you asking me? Why don't you ask somebody else? I am sick and tired of being the one who always says yes! Find somebody else for a change!" With that, she stormed up the stairs and slammed her bedroom door. Mercy threw herself on the bed and cried. She cried so hard that she did not hear Kate knocking gently on the door until it opened a crack. "What do you want? I told you no!"

"I'm not here about lunch, Mercy. I'm here because I am concerned about you. Do you want to talk?"

"No. I am done talking. I am done being nice and following the rules. It's just not worth it. Lily is right I am a goody two-shoes and where has it gotten me? I have no life. I have nothing and no one. My mother didn't want me. I don't even know my father. My sister doesn't want me and now, I can't have Timmy." She buried her face in the pillow and sobbed loudly.

Kate sat gingerly on the edge of the bed, relieved when Mercy did not object. After a few minutes, Mercy's crying subsided and she started to hiccup. She lifted her head. "What are you doing still here?"

"I thought you might need a friend," Kate said, waiting for the next flood of emotion.

"I have no friends," Mercy said, her face falling back into the wet pillow.

"I disagree," Kate said with confidence. "I can think of several people who care about you and would rally around you if needed." Mercy looked at her again and raised her eyebrows in question. "Well," Kate began, "me, for starters. And Leslie and Mike Barnes and even your social worker."

Mercy rolled her eyes. "Great. All professionals who are paid to be my friends. I told you I'm a loser!"

Kate smiled. "Those relationships might have started out that way, Mercy, when you were a kid. But I have seen those people change and become more important in your life. Now that you are an adult, we are all here because we want to be and not because we have to be. You have done a great job building a support system for yourself. All you have to do is ask for help and learn to trust it."

Mercy started to cry again. But these tears were different. Instead of feeling sorry for herself, she felt a tiny glimmer of hope. Instead of being angry, she felt relieved. Maybe they would help her. Lily had asked why Mercy always took their side. But, maybe, it was they who were on her side.

Chapter 28 *Ties That Bind*

Mercy tried to focus on what she was doing at work. But she was having difficulty. Her anxiety had been so high since the confrontation with Lily that she could hardly sleep at night. To make matters worse, tonight was her first shift at the hospital since the incident. She wanted to see Timmy more than ever, but she did not want to run into her sister again. Timmy's social worker from Child Services had called earlier. He was meeting with Lily today and he wanted to meet with Mercy tomorrow. Mercy had a lot of questions, but he couldn't answer them until he saw Lily. He would ask what her intentions were regarding Timmy. Whenever she thought about it, Mercy felt like she might throw up.

Finally, she couldn't stand it any longer. She asked her boss if she could leave an hour early. "Is everything okay, Mercy?" he asked. She nodded, not trusting her voice to answer without bursting into tears. She got to the hospital before she was expected and went directly to the NICU. Timmy was asleep, his monitors' lights blinking a steady beat. He no longer needed the feeding tube. Mercy was happy that he was growing stronger. But a little fear still tugged at the back of her mind, knowing there was no way she could be ready to take care of him, especially now that Lily had vowed to interfere. At least he still had the things that Mercy had brought in for him, as well as the things Barnes had given her. Standing by his isolette and looking at him in this peaceful state,

Mercy momentarily felt as if nothing had changed. He was still her Timmy.

She felt better about starting her shift in the ER after seeing Timmy. She got busy doing her routine chores and nobody bothered her, including Barnes, who was not working tonight. Mercy had been so reliable and unthreatening that the hospital staff no longer cared whether or not she was supervised. The nurses seemed to genuinely appreciate her help and had hinted that they hoped she would stay on, even after her community service requirement was satisfied. She hoped that her reputation wouldn't change, now that she was associated with Lily and her antics. Mercy still loved her sister and wanted what was best for her. But Lily was not making it easy. They had always been more than just half-sisters they had been allies. Surviving their mother's drinking, their fathers' absences and the never-ending foster homes was hard, but they faced it together whenever possible and Mercy looked out for her younger sister. But what could she do now that Lily did not want her help?

These questions nagged at her throughout her shift. When it ended, Mercy was exhausted, but decided to check in on Timmy again before heading home. Seeing him always raised her spirits and she hoped he would be awake this time. As she approached his room, Mercy stopped short in the corridor. The voice she heard coming from Timmy's room was unmistakably Lily's. She turned around and walked away, straight through the hospital lobby and all the way home.

When she reached the program, Mercy slipped in through the back door and went upstairs to her room. She wanted to cry, but no tears came. She felt completely empty inside as she sat on the edge of the bed, her hands in her lap. She wanted to talk to someone, but Kate wasn't working tonight. She did not have the nerve to call the hospital social worker or her Child Services social worker and besides, it was after hours and she would only get their voicemail. She had never called Barnes at home before and was afraid to disturb him. She remembered what Kate had said about people being on her side and wondered what good it was doing her now. Finally, she decided to call Leslie. Her next counseling appointment was not for three days, but she couldn't wait. And Leslie was the one person who was truly in her corner and had no ties or obligations to Lily. She left a message but knew that Leslie checked her work cell phone often and was likely to get it soon.

Mercy took a hot shower and tried to wash the day away. It left her feeling even more wiped out than before and she thought she'd skip eating dinner and go to bed. As she was pulling the covers back, her phone rang and she recognized Leslie's number on the caller ID. "What's up, Mercy?" she asked.

"I need to see you," Mercy said. "Things are not going well and I don't know what to do. Lily's back and everything has changed and she doesn't want me to have Timmy and the social workers have to talk to me tomorrow and I'm really scared." She finally burst into the tears that she had felt just beneath the surface all day.

"I'm so sorry, Mercy," Leslie said kindly. "Are you in crisis? I can meet you at the hospital in thirty minutes...."

"That's the last place I want to be!" Mercy shouted. "Besides, I just came from there!"

"Well, if it can wait until morning, we can meet at my office at eight o'clock. That way, you can get to work on time and I can still see my regular appointments. But you have to promise me that you will be safe tonight."

"I just want to sleep," Mercy sniffled, feeling the brief burst of emotion draining from her. "The morning sounds good."

After ending the call, Mercy realized that she was hungry. She went down to the kitchen for a snack before going to bed. Knowing that she would see her counselor first thing in the morning brought some hope and Mercy eventually fell into a deep sleep.

Chapter 29 *Always Have a Plan B*

She was ten minutes late for the appointment with Leslie, but the therapist was waiting with her office door ajar. Mercy fell into her usual chair and exhaled, looking miserable. "Where should we start?" Leslie asked. "When I saw you last, we talked about taking steps toward being the baby's primary caretaker."

"Well, we forgot the step where Lily shows up," Mercy said. She explained how she had discovered her sister at the hospital, recovering from a drug overdose. She described the confrontation when Lily had told Mercy to get out of her life as well as Timmy's. Mercy's voice shook as she recalled her conversation with the social worker and her anticipated meeting with him later today, after he spoke with Lily.

Leslie looked serious and was quiet for a moment. "I'm sorry that we didn't consider this possibility, Mercy," she said. "But it doesn't necessarily mean that you have to abandon your goal. Even if Lily does want to be a mother to Timmy, she is going to have to jump through a lot of hoops to satisfy Child Services and the court. Meanwhile, I think you should continue with your plan. Even if your sister is able to be a mother, Timmy is still going to need you in his life."

"But she hates me!" Mercy cried. "And I don't even know why."

"It sounds like Lily is being very defensive. And don't forget that she is withdrawing from drugs." Leslie paused. "I know your sister hurt you badly, Mercy. But have you considered how alone she is right now and how much she might need you?"

"She sure has a funny way of showing it!" Mercy blurted. "How am I supposed to help somebody who tells me to get out of her life?"

"Well, let's look at it from another perspective. What are your goals in this whole situation?" Leslie asked.

Mercy thought for a full minute before answering. "I want Timmy to grow up with family where he is loved. And I want my sister to be safe and off drugs. But I want to be part of both their lives, I want to take care of Timmy and have him grow up knowing he is safe, so he doesn't end up like me or like Lily."

"Okay...." Leslie said. "So, your goals for Lily have not changed. As long as I have known you, you have wanted her to be safe and drug-free, right?" Mercy nodded.

"And ever since Timmy was born, you have wanted the same thing for him," Leslie said. Mercy waited, not sure where this was leading and pretty sure she wasn't going to like it.

"I guess we should have acknowledged that you don't have control over what happens, Mercy. There are a lot of unknown factors and many people who will have a say in what happens to Timmy. But, even so, you can still move forward with your part and do what you need to do for Timmy. No one knows what Lily is going to do or what Child Services will recommend or even what the judge will decide. The only thing you can control is what Mercy is going to do. Try not to let this derail you."

She thought about it for a moment and wanted to argue, but everything Leslie said was true. She couldn't control Lily. She never could. She would have to continue with her own plans and wait to see what her sister was going to do. Her dreams might have been put on hold, but they were not necessarily out of reach. At least, not yet.

"But what if Lily won't let me see Timmy?" Mercy asked. "I couldn't bear that!"

"Talk to the social worker, Mercy. Let him know that your intentions have not changed. I can't imagine that he would allow Lily to end your relationship with the baby when you're the only one he has had all this time. And, besides, there needs to be a Plan B in case your sister cannot do it."

Mercy smiled. "I guess I'll have to be happy being Plan B, for now," she said. "Maybe Lily can live with that, too. But I am going to back off from her and let her have some space."

"I think that's a wise decision, too," Leslie said. "Let's meet again in a week and you can let me know what the social worker says."

Mercy headed to work, where she thought about the things Leslie had said. She knew it wasn't the ideal situation, but she felt she could live with it, for now. She tried to focus on the things she wanted to accomplish instead of on the things Lily had said to her at the hospital. And she had always wanted her sister to be here and to be safe. Somehow, Mercy needed to find a way to be happy about that.

Chapter 30 Good News / Bad News

When she came back from her lunch break, Mercy had a message from Timmy's social worker. She called back, taking deep breaths to calm her nerves. "I met with your sister this morning," he said. "Can you and I meet briefly this evening? I can come by the program."

Mercy agreed and the meeting was set for five-thirty. She hung up and tried not to think about it, but the afternoon was slow and she had plenty of time to make herself anxious. She wished she had her folder, with the notes from her last meeting at Child Services. She had been so confident and handled herself well.

On the bus ride home, Mercy decided that a repeat performance was just what she needed. Her ideas had not changed and she still planned to follow through with the parenting classes, probation requirements, and housing referral. She would still ask the nurses at the hospital to teach her everything she needed to know about Timmy's care. That, Mercy knew, was the one area where Lily could interfere. She had already prevented Mercy from visiting him once, without even knowing it. She hoped the social worker would be on her side on that point.

When she got to the program, she ran upstairs and grabbed her folder to fortify herself. She barely had time to review her notes before Timmy's social worker arrived. There was no one in the living room, so they sat on the worn couch, using the battered coffee table as a desk. "I saw Lily at the hospital this morning," he began. "And she has agreed to enter a day treatment program, for starters." Mercy tried to maintain a neutral expression. She struggled with conflicting emotions. This is what she had always prayed for. So, why did it feel like bad news?

He continued. "She agreed to allow me to tell you this, but it wasn't easy. She is pretty angry with you, Mercy. And now, she's angry with me, too." Mercy raised her eyebrows in question. "I suggested that it was in her best interest to re-establish her relationship with family so she would have support. And as far as I know, you are her only available family." Mercy smiled at the irony of Lily being asked to do the one thing she had vowed not to do to—let her help.

She finally found her voice and tried not to sound scared. "I've always wanted for my sister to get the help she needs," Mercy said. "But my feelings about Timmy are still the same. I am going to finish the parenting classes and visit Timmy at the hospital whenever I can."

"I think you should do all of the things you lined up for yourself. But you need to understand that I am obligated to offer your sister the same opportunities, since she is the biological mother. But she has a long way to go to prove herself. Her track record is not the greatest."

Mercy nodded. "I love my sister," she began, fighting back tears. "But I have to think about Timmy now."

"Very well said, Mercy. But I still want you to think about the possibility that Lily might succeed and think about whether or not you will be able to be a source of support for her. It's only fair to the baby that we try hard to give him a chance to be raised by his mother. But he will need you in his life, too, and so will Lily. Raising a child alone is a lot of work."

Mercy nodded in agreement and meant that she would at least consider it. But she wasn't sure she could do it. Not after the things Lily had said to her at the hospital. The words still stung. "Can Lily stop me from visiting the baby?" she asked, almost afraid to hear the answer.

"The baby is in state custody, so I have final say on those matters. You are on the visitors list for Timmy and I see no reason to change that. Lily will be starting her day treatment program at another hospital, so you should be able to see him during the day. Lily will be visiting at night."

Mercy was relieved to hear this, but wondered how in the world she was going to manage visiting Timmy during the day without missing work. Why wasn't anything ever easy? But she couldn't argue. She was grateful to have the social worker's support, even if he did want her to help Lily. Apparently, being Plan B had some strings attached.

Chapter 31 *It's Never Easy*

The next few days were a blur, as Mercy tried to stick to her routine and not think too much about Lily. It was difficult not knowing what her sister was doing, but she knew there was only so much the social workers could say, because of confidentiality. On a few occasions, she learned things from one of Timmy's nurses. Mercy would ask about his next feeding and the reply would be, "His mom gave him a bottle two hours ago." But now that Lily had been discharged from the hospital to start her drug treatment, even those hints were few and far between.

Mercy had to ask for time off during the day to visit the hospital, since Lily would be there in the evenings. She proposed taking a long lunch break two days a week, in exchange for working late or on Saturday mornings. Her boss nodded silently and looked at her thoughtfully, through steepled fingers. Mercy feared that he was going to say no. "I've been wondering how it was going," he finally said, "but didn't want to pry. My wife's best friend is a foster parent and I know something about it. The system can be frustrating, but the children really need people like her and like you." Mercy didn't know what to say. This was unexpected and she felt tears sting the back of her eyes. She managed to thank him without too much emotion and tried to flee before he showed her any more kindness. But before she reached the door, he spoke again. "I can rearrange the lunch schedules for Tuesdays and Thursdays, as long as you're only gone for ninety minutes. Not much goes on here evenings and weekends, so let's not worry about the time, for now."

She practically kicked up her heels on the way back to her desk. So many things had been a struggle lately that Mercy just anticipated everything would be a problem. She was giddy with relief when things went well. Now, if only her sister would come around. When Mercy started out on her path to take care of Timmy, she had never imagined that Lily would be her biggest obstacle. For years, Mercy had fantasized about the day her sister came back and got sober. But in her dreams, Lily was still the little sister who needed Mercy's protection. Now, Lily was almost an adult herself. And she was a mother—Timmy's mother. She had her own ideas about life. And Mercy didn't like it one bit.

At lunchtime, Mercy decided to walk through the mall to escape the thoughts that had filled her head all morning. She passed mothers pushing their babies in strollers. She paused to look at the window display of a store selling children's clothing. Instead of leaving her thoughts behind, Mercy felt worse. She was beginning to feel angry toward Lily. By the time she returned to work, she was wishing Lily would disappear again.

At five o'clock, Mercy practically ran to the bus stop. She needed to see Timmy. She convinced herself that Lily wouldn't be there tonight. Besides, Lily could see him every night, while she only had two hours a week it wasn't fair!

She approached Timmy's room cautiously. Peering around the doorway, Mercy found her favorite nurse diapering and dressing him. "Look who's here!" she said to the baby cheerfully. "It's Auntie!" Mercy's heart melted as the nurse placed a swaddled Timmy in her arms. "His mom won't be here until six o'clock, so you might as well rock him a bit. Oh—and he needs a burp." With that, she left them alone.

Mercy sat in the rocker and put Timmy on her shoulder, patting his back. He began to fuss and cry. She burst into tears, too. Even Timmy was fighting her, it seemed. She felt hopeless. Mercy didn't hear the footsteps enter the room behind her. "Whoa! What's happening here?" Barnes stood beside the rocker with his hands on his hips. "What's the matter, Mercy?" She stood abruptly and handed the baby to him. Reaching for a tissue, she turned away while she struggled to hide her embarrassment. Barnes jiggled Timmy expertly until he gave a loud burp, followed by a toothless grin. Even Mercy had to smile. She reached for Timmy and Barnes gave him up easily. "I'll let the nurse know he's ready for bed and then I'll buy you a cup of coffee," he said.

Alone again, Mercy held Timmy tight and breathed in his scent. "I love you," she whispered, and she kissed the side of his head. "And no one is ever going to take you away from me."

Chapter 32 Growing Pains

Mercy found a vacant table in the hospital cafeteria while Barnes got the coffees. Her sulking, bad mood was apparent on her face as he set the cups down and pulled out his chair. Mercy watched him, waiting until he was settled. "So, where have you been?" she asked. "I haven't seen you since forever!"

"I'm sorry, Mercy. I looked for you a couple of times last week, but our shifts don't always overlap anymore."

"That's because I can only visit Timmy during the day now. Lily gets to see him in the evening and there is no way I want to run into her."

"Actually, I saw her one night. She was giving him a bottle. She seemed a lot better than when she first came into the hospital. I couldn't believe it was the same girl."

"Oh, great! Another member of the Lily fan club. She just waltzes in here and decides it's time to be a mother and everybody is happy and forgets about me!"

"Wait a minute, Mercy. I was looking for you when I happened to see Lily. Besides, I thought you'd be thrilled to have your sister back. What's going on?"

Mercy sighed. "Oh, she's back, alright. And the only reason she wants Timmy is so I can't have him. She told me so herself. What if she fools everybody into letting her take him and then she takes off again or gets high and leaves him somewhere?"

"Whoa," he said. "You're getting a little ahead of yourself there. Nobody's going to let that happen. Lily has a long way to go before she gets to take that baby anywhere. If she gets to take him at all. You're not giving up, are you?"

"I might as well," Mercy said. "Everybody is on Lily's side. And I am totally out of it. I don't even know what she's doing."

Barnes looked at her. "Mercy, you're not going to do anything foolish, are you? You've worked so hard. Who knows what Lily is going to do? But, if she takes off again, that baby is going to need you."

Mercy sat quietly for a moment. Her sour mood was fading and she was grateful for Barnes being the voice of reason, as usual. She felt a little guilty for giving him a hard time. "Why are you always so nice to me?" she asked.

"Mercy, there is something I need to tell you. Then, maybe you'll understand why I say and do things. My grandmother raised me and I barely remember my mother. She had mental health problems and used drugs. I never had a father. Back then, Child Services was still new and laws didn't protect kids like they do now. If it wasn't for my grandmother, I don't know where I'd be, but I sure wouldn't be a police officer and I certainly wouldn't be sitting here giving you advice."

Mercy was dumbfounded. She had been so wrapped up in her own problems that it never occurred to her that Barnes might have his own. He was always so together and knew what to do. She had assumed it was because of his police training.

"Maybe when I look at you, I see what my mother might have been, with help," he continued. "Unfortunately, she was more like Lily. But maybe she could have taken care of me if she had the opportunity and some help like Lily."

"But what happened to your mother?" Mercy asked.

"She died when I was six, from a drug overdose."

They sat in silence for a few minutes while Mercy tried to digest what she had just learned. She thought about Lily. What if she did run away again and Timmy never got to know his mother? What if he had to learn that she was dead, like Barnes had? She imagined herself in his grandmother's shoes, being the one to break the news to him. She couldn't conceive anything worse.

Suddenly, she was standing and Barnes was speaking again. "Mercy, where are you going?"

"I have to find Lily and tell her I'm sorry, before it's too late!"

Chapter 33 Mike

Barnes convinced Mercy to sit down again, at least for a few minutes. "Let's think this through before you run off and have another big scene with your sister."

She agreed, mostly because she couldn't bear the thought of another fight with Lily. Besides, she didn't even know how to find her. "I'll have to catch her here at the hospital. I know she's visiting Timmy tonight!"

Barnes shook his head. "Do you really think it's a good idea to ambush her like that? Seeing you in the baby's room might set her off again."

Mercy chewed her lower lip. "All I know is that she's in a day treatment program somewhere. I don't even know where she's living."

"You're going to need some help with this, Mercy. Someone who can set it up and mediate. How about your social worker? Or Timmy's?"

"Right! They'll know where Lily is. And I know Timmy's worker wants her to see me." She pulled out her phone and called Child Services. The switchboard was closed for the day, so she left messages for both her social worker and Timmy's. She sat back, feeling deflated. "Now the waiting game begins."

"It will be worth it, Mercy. You don't want to mess this up—it's a big step."

Mercy drank her coffee and then asked, "Why didn't you tell me about your mother before?"

"When I first met you, I was always in a professional role, as a police officer. But, now that we're friends, I was waiting for the time to be right. I knew you didn't want to hear what I was saying tonight, about Lily, and I thought it might help if you understood where I was coming from."

"Thanks for telling me," she said. "It made me see things from a different perspective. I was so busy needing Timmy that I forgot all about Lily. She needs me to be her big sister again. And Timmy needs both of us right now. That will never happen if we're fighting."

Barnes smiled. "You've come a long way from the girl I found sleeping in the park, Mercy."

She blushed and didn't know what to say. She used to get angry or embarrassed when he teased her about that dreadful night. But Mercy knew he was right. She was no longer that shy girl who ran from things. These days, she was a girl with a plan.

"Time for me to be getting home. Can I give you a lift back to the program?"

"No, thanks. I think I'll walk home and think about what I'm going to say to my sister. But thanks again for everything, Officer Barnes."

"No problem, Mercy. And now that you know all my secrets, I think it's okay to call me Mike."

"Okay. Thanks, Mike."

She buttoned her jacket against the cool night air and headed home. Finally, she felt like she had some purpose, or at least a goal. If the social workers arranged a meeting with Lily, Mercy would apologize for not taking her sister's side. She would tell Lily how happy she was to have her back and how proud she was of her going to drug treatment. And she would ask about Timmy—no, about the baby. Lily's baby. That was going to be the hardest part. Mercy secretly hoped her sister would agree to let her call him Timmy. But, for now, she had to keep that just between them.

Chapter 34 *A Second Chance*

The first social worker to return her call was Timmy's. He was in favor of the meeting and promised to call again after he had spoken to Lily. Mercy's stomach was in knots again, but she was determined to follow through, despite the reoccurrence of her feelings that things were just not fair. Anything would be better than sneaking around to avoid Lily at the hospital and not having any idea what was going on with her sister. "But what if she doesn't go for it?" she had asked the social worker. "Well," he said, "I'm not just the baby's worker. Lily is also assigned to me and I am going to strongly recommend that she comply."

Great, Mercy thought. *One more reason for her to hate me.* So she was relieved when he called later the same day to say that it had been arranged. "I can't be there myself," he said. "I have to be in court on another case. But your sister's counselor at the drug program offered to handle it. She thinks your involvement is a good treatment goal for Lily." Mercy's relief was short-lived. It sure sounded like she was taking sides against her sister again. And now she had to deal with another counselor. Mercy hoped she was a normal person and not one of those 'touchy-feely' types.

The next day, she dressed carefully. She was beginning to wish she had more than one skirt. Between court and meetings, Mercy was tired of wearing the same outfit all the time. The knots in her stomach multiplied as she rode the bus to the stop nearest to Lily's day program. From there, it was a longer walk than she realized and she had to hurry.

Mercy arrived in a sweat and was glad to see the place was nice and sort of pretty. It was an old, Victorian home that had been converted to a mental health clinic. The receptionist was nice, too, and asked her to have a seat while she waited.

Lily's counselor was wearing jeans and she was very friendly. She made small talk on the way down the hallway to her office, where, she explained, Lily was already waiting. Mercy was practically shaking by the time they reached the small, windowless room. The counselor entered first. "Lily? Your sister is here." She opened the door wide to let Mercy into the room.

Lily looked up from an easy chair. Mercy took in the shiny blonde hair, clear complexion and bright eyes. Mike Barnes was right—she looked nothing like the girl from the hospital! She looked like Lily again, only older. She was still thinner than Mercy remembered, but she looked healthy. After a moment, the counselor invited Mercy to sit and then she took a seat behind her desk. "Let's begin." She smiled and looked at Lily expectantly. For the first time, the sisters' eyes met. Mercy tried to smile without coming on strong. Lily dropped her eyes. Her hands fidgeted in her lap. Finally, she took a breath and sat on her hands to keep them still.

"Thanks for coming," Lily began. "And thank you for taking care of my baby while I was gone." Mercy couldn't believe her ears. Lily continued, sounding rehearsed, but Mercy didn't care. "I'm sorry for the way I behaved when you came to see me in the hospital." She stole a quick glance at Mercy, then Lily's gaze returned to her lap.

"Mercy," the counselor said, "would you like to respond to Lily?" She wished she had written down what she planned to say. Her sister's words had taken her by surprise and it took Mercy a moment to gather her thoughts.

"I'm sorry, too. I should have listened to you that day. I should have told you that I'm glad you came back and that you are getting help." Mercy looked at the counselor, hoping for some direction. Lily still wouldn't look at her.

"One of the goals Lily has set for herself is to build a support system, to help her parent her son. Isn't that right, Lily?" the counselor asked.

Mercy looked at Lily, who nodded in reply. Without lifting her head, she raised her eyes to meet Mercy's. "Will you help me?"

"Yes, of course!" Mercy said. "You and Ti—the baby—are all I have! You are my only family."

Lily smirked. "His name is Bo."

Mercy felt like she'd been stabbed in the heart. But she tried to hide it because Lily was looking at her for the first time, as if gauging her reaction. "Okay," was all she could manage.

"So," the counselor said, in an obvious attempt to rescue the moment. "How can your sister help, Lily? Can you be more specific about what that might look like?"

Lily shrugged her shoulders. "I guess you could visit me at my foster home? And maybe help me figure out things I'm going to need for Bo."

Mercy softened at the invitation, however tentative. At least she'd have some input in Timmy's life. "That would be awesome," she said, with forced cheerfulness. "Give me the address and let me know when to come."

Lily looked at the counselor again, as if to indicate she was done. Mercy wasn't sure what to think. It seemed like there was a lot more to say. But at least this was a start, even if it was an awkward one. The counselor handed them each a pen and a yellow sticky pad so they could exchange contact information. Once that was accomplished, Lily left the room without a good-bye. The counselor escorted Mercy back to the lobby and thanked her for coming.

Back on the street, Mercy felt unsatisfied. She thought over all the things that Lily had said. The words were right, but Mercy found little comfort because of the way Lily had delivered her lines: like she had decided what her counselor expected her to say and memorized it. The whole meeting had been uncomfortable, to say the least. But, at least she didn't shout nasty things at Mercy, like the last time they met.

Instead of visiting Timmy, like she had planned, Mercy decided to head straight home. She just couldn't face him now that things had changed. And she certainly couldn't call him by any other name.

Chapter 35 Coming to Terms

A few days went by before she heard from Lily. Mercy still couldn't bring herself to visit Timmy and she really missed him. Plans were made for her to visit Lily at her foster home the following day, right after work. She sounded more like herself on the telephone and Mercy thought maybe it was the counselor who made Lily act that way. Maybe things would be better when they were alone.

She decided to see Timmy at lunchtime the next day. She needed some peace before seeing Lily again and she thought seeing him would do the trick. At lunchtime, Mercy walked as quickly as she could to the hospital. Timmy was in a regular crib now. She leaned over the crib and his blue eyes met hers. Mercy melted. She lifted him and held him close for a moment. A flood of emotions coursed through her. His warmth and scent were so familiar. But Mercy knew things were different now. She would always be his aunty, but she was no longer the most important person in his life. That position belonged to Lily now.

A nurse came in with a warmed bottle and handed it to Mercy. "He'll be going home soon!" she said cheerfully. Mercy wondered where home would be for Timmy. It wouldn't be with her. Afterward, as she rocked him and he dozed contently, Mercy felt the loss. It felt as if she was holding him for the last time. That wasn't true, but it was the last time she would think of Timmy as hers. A single tear slipped from her eye and slid down her cheek.

As she walked back to work, Mercy found the peace she had been seeking. She was still sad. But she realized that it was not so much her role in Timmy's life that mattered—it was just his presence in hers. She prom-ised herself that she would try her hardest to support Lily. By doing so, she would not only have her sister back, but she would remain close to Timmy. Or Bo. Mercy cringed. Some things were not going to be so easy.

When she got to the foster home that evening, Lily answered the door. She introduced Mercy to her foster mother, who seemed nice enough. When she showed Mercy her room, the sisters were alone for the first time in at least a year. "So. How do you like living here?" Mercy asked.

"They're nice, I guess," Lily said. "But they're new at this and they have a lot of rules. They do everything my social worker tells them and they're always looking at me weird, like I'm going to light myself on fire or some-thing." Both girls laughed.

"How about your social worker?" Mercy asked.

"Ugh. He's always telling me what to do and running out the door be-cause he's got better things to do. He says Bo has to live in a different foster home, even though they have room for him here. What a jerk. I can't even see my own baby unless he says so."

Mercy didn't know what to say. She understood the social worker's decisions but didn't want Lily to think she was taking sides against her. Lily was looking at her as if she was challenging Mercy to do just that. "Really? That's not right," Mercy lied, with as much conviction as she could. "How will you see him at all, once he's out of the hospital?" She was asking for herself more than for Lily.

"Supervised visits only," Lily said, sarcastically mimicking the social worker. "I have to go to Child Services so he can watch me and I only get an hour a week. It's bullshit."

Mercy's heart sank. If his mother only gets an hour a week, how was she ever going to see him? She couldn't ask Lily that question, so she kept it to herself.

Lily showed her another small room, where she had stored some baby things. Mostly, there were cute outfits and a pair of little cowboy boots. Someone had given Lily a used car seat that needed to be cleaned and a couple of homemade baby blankets. Mercy was not impressed, although Lily seemed quite proud of herself. "I don't have a crib yet, but as soon as I get a job, I can buy one."

"Don't you have to stay in the day program?" Mercy asked.

"Only for another four weeks, if I pass my drug screens," Lily said. "The stupid social worker thinks I'm going back to school to a teen parenting program. But there's no way! I just need a job so I can take care of Bo by myself."

Mercy just nodded in agreement. She didn't trust herself to speak, knowing she couldn't hide her true feelings. Lily had her own ideas about things. But at least she was talking to her. Mercy would have to keep quiet if she wanted to keep an eye on her sister. And on Timmy.

Chapter 36 *You're Free to Go*

Mercy was busy at work the next day and managed not to think about Lily, for a change. Her mind was far from her own problems when she answered the phone and was surprised to hear her social worker's voice. "I'm sorry to bother you at work," she said. "But I've been asked for a status report for your court appearance tomorrow and needed to check in with you." Mercy froze. Court? She had forgotten all about it! Quickly, she looked at her calendar and there it was, written in the square for the next day. Mercy had been so preoccupied thinking about Timmy that she hadn't realized it. "Will you be there?" she asked the social worker. "I can't attend the hearing, but I spoke with your court appointed attorney and he will be there with you. You're in good shape, Mercy, so it shouldn't be a problem."

Yeah, right! Mercy thought. *Things have not exactly been going my way lately.* But she confirmed that she would be there before hanging up. Now she had something else to worry about. When would it end?

She took her nice outfit out of the closet when she got home that night and thought, *I really need to go shopping!* But it would have to do, for now.

The next morning, she dressed and grabbed a bagel from the kitchen before heading out the door. It was raining hard and Mercy shivered beneath her umbrella at the bus stop. She got to court in time and looked for her lawyer. The halls were crowded with other people who were obviously doing the same thing. She was about to give up when she heard her name shouted out at the end of the corridor. Mercy fought her way through the bodies and walked in the direction of the male voice, which sounded angry. When she finally got there, she was greeted by her probation officer, who indicated that he wanted her to enter his office. Once inside, she was relieved to be out of the chaos. He was his usual gruff self, but his office was quiet and cool.

Mercy sat in a hard chair and the PO took a seat behind his desk. Opening a folder, he barely looked up. "Looks like everything's in order. Good reports from your employer, Child Services, and your shelter program. Fines are up to date. You still owe court fees. But we can take care of that later." He finally looked up and seemed surprised to find her still there. Mercy didn't know what to say. Besides, he already knew everything about her. "Is your lawyer here?" he asked.

"I couldn't find him, but he's supposed to be," she said.

Next thing Mercy knew, she was being ushered back out into the sweaty hallway. She squeezed into an empty spot on a bench and waited. Everyone was talking at once and it gave her a headache. Mercy felt out of place and decided that was a good thing. For a brief moment, she envied her sister. Lily, she thought, would be more at home in a place like this.

She felt a shadow over her and looked up. Her lawyer was standing there, motioning her to follow him. Again, Mercy struggled through the sea of bodies, trying to follow the attorney. He stopped at the very end of the corridor and leaned against the wall, facing a corner. This, Mercy supposed, is what qualified as privacy.

"How's it going, Mercy?" he asked, flipping through his notes distractedly.

"Fine, I guess," she said, not sure how to answer.

"What's this about parenting classes?" He was pointing to a document on fancy paper: the social worker's report! Mercy almost groaned out loud.

"My sister had a baby. I was doing it for him."

"Impressive," the lawyer said. "Says you are being considered as a possible resource for the baby?"

117

Mercy nodded, hoping to avoid the gory details of Lily's return.

Before he could ask another question, someone was yelling the attorney's name and he hurried back into the courtroom. Mercy found another place on another bench and waited.

Finally, the door to the courtroom opened and she heard her name called. Mercy walked in, trying to look like she knew what she was doing. Her lawyer was seated at a long table and pulled a chair out for her. The judge was on the bench—the same judge she had seen the last time. Her probation officer sat across the room. He stood, still holding the folder that contained her life story. *Here we go again*, she thought, bracing herself to hear all about her embarrassing history.

But, when she finally focused on his words, the PO was telling the judge that she no longer required court supervision. Her remaining fees, he said, could be collected without Mercy being on probation. This sounded good!

Next, her attorney stood. "Your Honor," he began. "My client has no prior record and has been in no trouble since this unfortunate incident. In fact, she is working with Child Services to become a resource for her sister's child. I ask that the charges be dropped and the court fees waived at this time."

The judge looked at Mercy. "Well done, young lady. Don't ever let me see you in my courtroom again!" He banged his gavel and everyone shuffled their papers and stood up and the judge left the room. "What just happened?" she asked her lawyer.

"You're free to go, Mercy. No more probation and no more restitution. You're done here. Good luck."

Outside, Mercy took a deep breath of fresh air. The sun was out and the world looked better than it had in days, maybe weeks. She put away her umbrella and decided to walk to work. But first, she'd treat herself to a large iced coffee.

Chapter 38 *A Sight for Sore Eyes*

Mercy's happiness was short-lived. Her social worker called again the next day. She asked about court and congratulated Mercy on her probation being over. But there was something in her voice that told Mercy she hadn't called to celebrate. "I want to let you know that Lily's baby is being discharged from the hospital today. His foster parents are there right now, learning about his care." Her heart sank. She knew this day was coming, but needed more time to prepare.

"How will I see him now?" she asked.

"You're on the approved visitors list, Mercy. But it might take a while. The foster parents have a lot to do and will be setting up a visitation schedule with Lily first. But they have agreed to let you visit him in their home. Be patient."

She hung up and stared at the phone for a few moments. Mercy knew she should be happy that Timmy was doing so well and leaving the hospital. But somehow, good news was making her sad these days. First Lily coming home and now Timmy finding a new family. She remembered what Leslie had said. Both were things she had wished for. She needed to think of the events as positive, even if they weren't happening as she had imagined them.

Now that her probation terms had been met, Mercy's community service at the hospital was also over. It's just as well, she thought. She couldn't bear to be there now and not see Timmy. The only thing Mercy had to keep her busy in the evenings was the parenting class. Her social worker had found a course that was child development-based. The other students in the group were young parents or future foster parents. She wondered why Lily wasn't taking the classes. Maybe she was too busy.

This week's class was about newborns and how they learned to recognize their primary caretaker. Mercy was devastated to think that Timmy was bonding with a complete stranger. Would he even know who she was anymore? Had he even gotten to know Lily in the short time she'd been back? She had so many questions. But she couldn't bring herself to ask them. She wasn't sure she wanted to hear the answers.

It was hard to imagine what Timmy's life was like now. She tried to imagine him with a pair of foster parents in the class. They were nice enough. Did they dress him in someone else's baby clothes? Did they know how he liked to be rocked to sleep after his bottle? Worst of all, what did they call him?

The rest of the week dragged slowly. Mercy was dreading the weekend, with no hospital work and no visits to Timmy. Hanging around the program was not something she was used to doing any more. Then, Friday, the foster mother called and invited Mercy to visit! She could hardly sleep, her excitement keeping her awake much of the night. She dressed and ran down the stairs early the next morning. Kate was in the kitchen, making coffee. "What's up, Mercy?" she asked. "I didn't expect anybody up for a while."

She talked so fast that Kate had trouble keeping up, but Mercy filled her in on the week's news, including court, Timmy's discharge, and her plans to visit him today at the foster home. "Wow!" Kate said. "You've had quite a week!" Mercy smiled. It had seemed like such a long week, but now she realized that quite a lot had happened, after all.

"What do you know about the foster parents?" Kate asked.

"Not much. But I have to take two buses to get there. It's kind of far. I just hope they're nice and keep letting me visit."

"The girls made cookies yesterday. Do you want to take some to the visit?" Kate asked. Mercy liked the idea and put five cookies on a small plate. She covered them with plastic wrap before heading to the bus stop.

She was a bundle of nerves and excitement. But she managed to make the right connection for the second bus and arrived with the cookies intact. Taking a breath to calm her nerves, Mercy rang the doorbell.

The woman who answered the door was older than she had imagined. She had short, graying hair and a warm smile. "You must be Aunt Mercy! I'm Pat," she said, offering her hand, which Mercy shook and awkwardly gave her the cookies. "Come on in! Bo is waiting for you! He's on the dining room floor, having some tummy time." She was so happy to be there that Mercy couldn't even cringe at the name. She followed Pat around the corner to the next room, where Timmy was lying on a thin blanket that had been spread on the carpet. Pat scooped him up, planting a kiss on his cheek, and handed him to Mercy.

She held him against her, face to face, for a moment, and then held him at arm's length, to get a good look at him. "I'll make us some tea to go with these cookies," Pat said, leaving them alone. Mercy saw an old rocker in the corner and sat with the baby in her arms. He was chubbier, she thought, and dressed in an adorable blue outfit. He gazed back at her, looking content.

As she rocked, Mercy checked out the new surroundings. There were lots of pictures on the wall, mostly school portraits of a boy and a girl, recognizable as they grew up in the series of framed photos. Pat returned, carrying two mugs of tea, and caught her looking. "Those are our kids," she said. "They're both grown now. Our daughter is married and our son is in college. We adopted them both through Child Services." Before Mercy could react, Pat continued. "Nowadays we take mostly newborns. But we're done adopting. We've had 52 babies in the past ten years!"

Mercy was relieved that there were no plans to adopt Timmy. She sipped her tea and talked with Pat about the program, her job, and about Lily. Pat seemed to know a lot about how things worked and asked Mercy questions that were easy to answer. Mercy even told her how she couldn't bring herself to call him Bo, having named him Timmy before Lily came back. "I like Timmy much better, too," Pat said. "But, for now, I have to use the name his mother gave him." As if on cue, he started fussing and Pat let Mercy change him and put him to bed. He had his own room and a nice crib.

Before leaving, Mercy arranged to visit again the following Saturday. At the door, Pat gave her a hug and thanked her for coming. As she walked back toward the bus stop, Mercy was finally able to feel genuinely happy for Timmy. He looked so healthy and his foster mother really seemed to care about him. It was much easier to think about him, now that she had a picture in her mind of his new home. Lily, however, was another story. Mercy still wasn't sure what was going on with her sister. But for now, everybody was safe. That was all she could ask for.

Chapter 38 *Never a Dull Moment*

Mercy didn't hear from Lily for a couple of weeks. She had called and left messages at her foster home, but Lily had not called back. She knew that Lily had been visiting with the baby at the Child Services office every week because Pat talked about taking Timmy to the visits. But other than that, she had no information. Mercy fell into the routine of working, seeing Timmy on Saturdays and going to parenting group and counseling. Sometimes, she felt like there was something she was forgetting to do. It had been awhile since her life was drama-free and she was having trouble getting used to it!

One day, she was eating lunch at the mall food court during her lunch break when she heard a familiar voice. "Well hello, stranger!" She looked up to find a friendly face, but it took her a moment to recognize it.

"Mike!" she said. "I hardly knew you without the uniform! What are you doing here?"

"I had some shopping to do so I'm spending my precious day off here, with my wife and son. I'm meeting them for lunch, if they remember. How about you, Mercy? I haven't seen you at the hospital and I went looking for you, but Timmy had been discharged. What's going on?"

She brought him up to date on the Lily story. He listened, while scanning the area for his family. "Sounds like everything is on course," he said when she was finished.

"I guess so," Mercy said. "But, to tell you the truth, it's kind of boring."

"You know," Mike said, "everybody at the hospital has been asking about you. You can always come back as a regular volunteer." He started waving his arms frantically and Mercy saw a woman pushing a stroller headed toward them. When they arrived, he introduced Mercy to his wife and two-year-old son.

She smiled warmly and said, "It's nice to meet you, Mercy. I've heard so many great things about you." Mercy blushed. His wife was pretty, just like she imagined her to be. She was glad that Mike had such a nice family.

"I need to get back to work," she said, cleaning up the remnants of her lunch.

"Well, don't be a stranger," Mike said. "And think about what I said. Maybe I'll see you at the hospital again soon."

She waved good-bye to the Barnes family and headed back to work. But she thought about what he had said. Mercy realized that she missed the hospital more than she was willing to admit. So much had happened there that it felt like her second home. After Timmy left, she couldn't bear it. But now that she was spending time with him at the foster home every weekend, it didn't matter.

And Mercy was happy that Timmy was where he was. She could see him growing stronger and bigger every week. But, it was getting harder to leave him. Pat usually let her do everything when she was there. She fed him, changed him, and even bathed him. Pat stayed nearby, but didn't interfere except for an occasional suggestion. For two wonderful hours a week, Timmy, not Bo, was her baby again.

This Saturday, after visiting Timmy, she decided to head to the hospital and ask about coming back to work. The charge nurse was happy to see her and excited about the possibility of her returning. She sent Mercy to the coordinator of volunteer services. Her original application was still on file. Mercy was surprised to learn that her work had been evaluated by the ER nurse manager. She had received high marks and praise. So, she was excused from the usual volunteer orientation. She could resume her previous duties whenever she was ready.

Mercy was deep in thought on her way home from the hospital, thinking about her decision to return to volunteering and looking forward to getting started. Passing beneath a railroad bridge, she was startled out of her daydream by movement in the shadows of the overpass. The location was known for trouble at night, but Mercy had never seen anything happen during the day and she walked this same route on a regular basis. She tried to keep her head down and walk faster, but there was something familiar about one of the forms in the dark corner. She looked closer, squinting into the shadows.

"Lily?" she shouted, before the thought had finished forming in her mind. Mercy caught a quick glimpse of her sister's face before Lily started running in the opposite direction, dropping something as she went. The others in her little group followed. Mercy began running too, but was too far behind to catch up. She stopped where Lily had been standing and looked down. There, on the broken concrete, was a pipe. And it was still burning.

She kicked some sand over the pipe and walked away. Her mind raced about what to do next. Mercy walked the rest of the way home with her fists clenched inside her pockets. She was furious with Lily for using drugs again. *No wonder she didn't return my calls*, Mercy thought. She was angry with herself for not seeing it coming. And now she had to figure out what she was going to do about it.

Chapter 39 A New Dilemma

When she arrived back at the program, the decision was made for her. She had a message to call Lily's foster mother. "She said it's an emergency," Kate told her as she handed Mercy a scrap of paper with the number. She ran upstairs, where she returned the call in the privacy of her room.

Mercy, thanks for calling," said Lily's foster mother. "I was wondering if you had heard from your sister today. She didn't come home after day treatment, like she always does, and I know you keep in touch with her."

What? Mercy was confused. "Actually, she never calls me back," she told the woman.

"I had no idea, Mercy," she said. "I gave her your messages and just assumed..."

Now Mercy was angry again and it gave her the push to talk about what she had seen. "I saw Lily on my way home, just a little while ago," she said. "She was under the bridge on South Main Street with three other people and it looked pretty shady." She just couldn't rat her sister out completely.

"That doesn't sound good," the foster mother said. "I'd better call her social worker."

Mercy ended the call and stared at the blank screen. The anger had drained from her and she started to worry. How was Lily going to get out of this? She was sure that she had to have drug screens as part of her deal with Child Services. What a mess.

An hour later, Lily's social worker called. "I'm asking the court for a runaway warrant on Lily," he said. "I know you saw her today, Mercy. The police need to take your statement. Is it okay to send the officer over to see you tonight?"

Mercy agreed, even though she was not thrilled with the idea of ratting her sister out again. *But what choice do I have?* She thought. Mercy knew this would probably stop Lily from seeing Timmy. She couldn't stand the idea of her having Timmy if she wasn't serious about staying clean and sober. Lily didn't make good decisions and she didn't hang out with the best people when she was using. Mercy hoped she could do the right thing when she talked to the police officer. Even if she could, she knew that she was never going to feel good about it.

The officer who came to talk to her was all business. Mercy figured he thought anybody who lived in the program was no different than the runaway he was investigating. "Are you sure it was your sister?" he asked, tapping his pencil against his notebook. That's when she remembered him. He was here the night that Jess was arrested, after Mercy found the stolen jewelry in her room. And he was just as miserable then as he was now.

"I saw her face," Mercy told him. "And she ran when I called her name. I think I know my own sister."

"Is there anything else you can tell me?"

Mercy looked away. She had not yet included the part about the pipe. She debated quickly and decided only to tell Lily's social worker. That way, he could have her drug-tested before she saw Timmy again. But maybe the police wouldn't arrest Lily when they found her.

The officer left without saying thank you. Mercy was exhausted. She went to her room, threw herself on the bed, and stared at the ceiling. So much for leading a boring life, she thought.

Chapter 40 *The Solution*

The next day, Mercy went to work, but her mind was on Lily. Everytime the phone rang, she held her breath, convinced it was one of the social workers or Lily's foster mother, with news. But no one called. Finally, at four o'clock, she couldn't stand it any longer. She called Lily's social worker and had to leave a message on his voicemail. An hour later, she was close to tears when she finally heard from back from him. "I would have called you earlier," he said, "but I've been in meetings all day."

"Where's Lily?" Mercy asked.

"We don't know, Mercy. She was supposed to meet Pat and the baby at the pediatrician's yesterday, for the baby's well visit, but she was a no-show. She was also absent from her day treatment and never came home, as you know."

Mercy felt sick. "But I saw her yesterday! She was right there. Can't you do something?"

"The police are watching for her, Mercy, but if she relapsed and is using again, she's not going to want us to find her."

Lily was gone. Lily was gone again. And they weren't going to do anything about it. Just like when her mother went away. Mercy was only a little girl, but she'd never forget. Her mother got out of jail and simply disappeared, leaving her alone. And now it was happening again. But this time, she told herself, she wasn't alone. "What about Timmy?" she asked. "What's going to happen to him?"

"We'd actually like to talk with you about that, Mercy. Is it okay if your social worker and I come by later, when you get out of work?"

Her heart skipped a beat. This couldn't be good, if they were both coming to tell her in person. "I'll be home in a half hour," Mercy said.

The trip home was the longest bus ride of her life. Mercy tried not to let her imagination run wild, but she was scared. Lily was gone and now she was going to lose Timmy, too. It was too much. She finally reached the program just as the two social workers pulled into the driveway. Mercy passed the other residents in the kitchen and the living room without answering their greetings. She went straight to the office, glad to find it empty. The social workers followed and they all found seats. Mercy thought she'd faint if they didn't get to the point.

"I'm sorry about Lily," her social worker began. "If she comes back, we'll start over and offer her the same services as before. But she won't be able to see her baby until she has maintained sobriety and stability for a longer period of time." Mercy could only stare at her. "We met with our administration today, about the baby," she continued. "We don't think it's fair for him to wait indefinitely in foster care. He deserves a chance to have a permanent family."

Here it comes, thought Mercy, bracing herself.

Lily's social worker spoke next. "I had made a referral for your sister," he said, "for a young parents program. She could live there, with the baby. But that's no longer an option." Mercy thought her heart would break in two.

"There's going to be an opening next week," he said, "and Lily had been accepted into the program. We're hoping that you might take the spot, instead of your sister."

She must have heard them wrong. "What did you just say?"

The social workers both chuckled. "We want you to consider going into the young parents program, with Lily's baby," he said, speaking more slowly so Mercy could absorb the idea.

"It's a pretty unusual situation," her social worker said. "But you've worked so hard, Mercy, and I know we talked about this possibility before Lily came back. We worked it out for you to transfer to the new program, with the baby. If it goes well, you can petition the court for custody when you've completed the program."

Mercy burst into tears. Then she started laughing. She stood up. She sat back down. She couldn't form any words, but the emotion poured out of her.

"We'll take that as a yes," her social worker said.

Epilogue

Timmy finally gave in to sleep just after midnight. Mercy tiptoed from the room and collapsed onto the couch. She was certain that everyone else in the program was asleep, parents and babies alike. Reaching over to the end table, she turned on the monitor again, relieved to hear only the steady rhythm of his breathing. She had planned to shower before bed, but now, she was just too tired. Mercy folded her legs up and hugged her knees to her chest. Her head fell back against the lumpy cushion and she looked around the small living room. The bare walls stared back at her. Someday, she thought, she would hang some pictures and make it look pretty. For now, the only color in the room was a plastic laundry basket filled with baby toys. She was okay with that. More than okay, really. Mercy was proud. And despite being exhausted most of the time, she was happy.

The only thing she had done that could pass for decorating was to place three small photos on the end table. The staff at the old program had given her some frames from the dollar store as a going-away gift. She picked up the first, an old photo of her mother. It wasn't much, but it was all she had and enough to help her remember. The next was the first picture she had taken of Timmy, with her phone, in the hospital. Mercy had found comfort in that little photo many times, when things were not going well and the future was uncertain. Now, it reminded her of how far they both had come.

The last picture was of Mercy and Lily. They were sitting on a couch, with their arms around each other, smiling at the camera. She couldn't remember where it had been taken or by whom. But it told a story of two sisters who clung to one another, no matter where life took them. There had been some good times. But, growing up in foster care felt mostly like a series of bad times and worse times. Mercy wanted Timmy to have only good memories.

She dusted the frame off, using the hem of her tee shirt, and placed it back on the end table. She wondered where Lily was now and if she ever remembered those days, when she would crawl into Mercy's bed, in a strange place, in the middle of the night and cry herself to sleep. Years of counseling had taught her that it wasn't her fault. Mercy had been a child herself back then. How could she have known how to keep her sister safe?

When Timmy was older, he would learn about his family through these faded photographs. He would know where he came from. He would help Mercy remember more of the good times. Together, they would make their own family history and she would take more happy pictures.

Mercy still hoped that Lily might come home again someday, that they might make room in Timmy's life for his real mother. But that was up to Lily and she'd have to be clean and sober. Right now, that felt like a long shot. She still caught glimpses of her sister now and then, on busy streets or on a crowded bus. Leslie said it was just Mercy's subconscious trying to accept Lily's disappearance. But Mercy liked to imagine that her sister was close by, watching over her and Timmy. It was a lot easier than thinking about the alternative.

She wondered if Lily loved Timmy and, if she did, how she could walk away. These were the same questions Mercy had always asked herself about her own mother. She had believed that, if she was good, her mother would come home. Somehow, she had to make sure Timmy didn't grow up with the same idea. She would make sure that he knew he was loved, no matter what.

But, for right now, Mercy needed to get some rest. She turned off the lights and carried the portable monitor into her bedroom. Before long, her own breathing seemed to echo the sound of Timmy's and she drifted off to sleep. Tomorrow would come quickly and there would be time to think about her crazy family and to show Timmy that, despite it all, he was loved.

About The Author

Barbara Ann Whitman is a seasoned social worker with experience as a child abuse and neglect investigator. She has worked professionally with hundreds of foster children. Currently, she is employed by a nonprofit agency that empowers foster children to become successful adults.

Her short story "A Changing Sea" was published in the anthology *Shoreline* and her poem "Galilee" was featured in the book *Under the Thirteenth Star*.

She has been a Sunday School teacher, a Youth group Leader, a parenting instructor, a Big Sister and a Girl Scout Leader. Barbara Ann founded a Meetup Group for active seniors in 2015. She is a member of the Old Fiddlers Club of Rhode Island and sings in her church choir.

This is her first novel.

Made in the USA
Lexington, KY
10 September 2018